Anything to Do with You!"

Stephanie said with as much firmness as she could muster.

"Don't you?" Pierre's tone was mocking, but there was a grim look about his eyes that did nothing to allay the panic within her. There had to be a way to put him in his place once and for all! She had to cut off the dangerous flow of electricity between them!

He gave her no time to think about it. The pressure of his hands brought her up tight against him. She was paralysed by her unwitting response to him and trembled in his arms.

"All or nothing, *cherie*," he murmured against her lips. "Make up your mind—"

ELIZABETH HUNTER
uses the world as her backdrop. She paints with broad and colorful strokes, yet she is meticulous in her eye for detail. Well known for her warm understanding of her characters, she is internationally beloved by her loyal and enthusiastic readers.

Dear Reader:

I'd like to take this opportunity to thank you for all your support and encouragement of Silhouette Romances.

Many of you write in regularly, telling us what you like best about Silhouette, which authors are your favorites. This is a tremendous help to us as we strive to publish the best contemporary romances possible.

All the romances from Silhouette Books are for you, so enjoy this book and the many stories to come.

Karen Solem
Editor-in-Chief
Silhouette Books

ELIZABETH HUNTER
Loving Relations

Silhouette Romance

Published by Silhouette Books New York

America's Publisher of Contemporary Romance

SILHOUETTE BOOKS a Division of Simon & Schuster, Inc.
1230 Avenue of the Americas, New York, N.Y. 10020

Distributed by Pocket Books

ISBN: 0-671-57310-1

First Silhouette Books Printing August, 1984

10 9 8 7 6 5 4 3 2 1

Map by Ray Lundgren

America's Publisher of Contemporary Romance

Printed in the U.S.A.

BC91

Books by Elizabeth Hunter

Silhouette Romance

The Lion's Shadow #18
Bride of the Sun #51
A Touch of Magic #65
Written in the Stars #91
One More Time #137
A Silver Nutmeg #167
London Pride #198
Fountains of Paradise #218
Shared Destiny #240
A Tower of Strength #257
Kiss of the Rising Sun #268
A Time to Wed #278
Rain on the Wind #290
Song of Surrender #298
Loving Relations #310

For Monica,
my sister-in-law

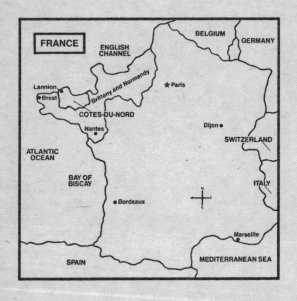

Chapter One

Despite the favourable time of year it was not the best day she could have chosen to make the Channel crossing. Nor was she a particularly good sailor. She had tried the lounge and had found it wanting, and now she was standing on the open deck, staring down at the almost black sea below. Every time the bow rose and fell, she braced her knees, waiting for the drenching spray that came up over the deck and the spot where she was standing. Halfway over and she was soaked to the skin, no longer pretending to enjoy the brief interlude between Dover and Boulogne.

There was plenty to look at—the Straits of Dover are the busiest shipping lane in the world. Overhead the gulls screamed and competed with each other for the scraps that were being thrown into the sea from a platform down below. They sounded as bad-tempered as she felt.

She had started out quite pleased with her appearance; her blouse was pretty, if inexpensive, and her cord trousers were of a glorious rust colour that had hardly been improved by the wetting they had received. Worse, her champagne-coloured, naturally highlighted hair hung round her neck in strands, and any makeup she had put on to accentuate the emerald green of her finely shaped eyes had long since been washed off. All in all, she felt a mess.

"Come below, mademoiselle, and I'll buy you a coffee!"

Stephanie Ironside jumped, and turned to see who had accosted her. He could have doubled for a pirate anytime. He was tall, black-haired and with skin that had seen more sun than Northern Europe had for a long, long time. His clothes matched his image, a pair of white trousers and a scarlet knitwear shirt that opened far enough for her to be able to see that his tan was not only on his face.

"I think I'm better off where I am," she answered, also in French.

"You're getting very wet."

"Very."

He came and stood beside her, leaning on the rails and staring down at the sea as she had been doing.

"I do not think you'll feel better this way. Come, let's get out of the wind and the spray at least."

He touched her on the hand, his finger warm and determined. Stephanie was totally unprepared for her own reaction, which struck her as being wholly inappropriate. Fortunately, he could not have known of the sudden weakness in her knees, nor of the lurching feeling inside her—though that might have had a quite different cause.

She allowed herself to be led to a more sheltered spot where, to her surprise, a pale beam of sunlight had broken through the leaden clouds above and was doing its best to warm up the only vacant seat.

He stood over her for a long moment, looking her up and down. The heavy lids of his eyes gave him a lazy look, but there was nothing lazy about the dark eyes beneath. They, she was sure, missed nothing in their scrutiny of her appearance.

She shivered, embarrassed. "You're right. This is better," she acknowledged politely. "I think I may survive after all." Once again she spoke in French and saw that he registered the fact, storing the incident away as if it were something he wanted to remember sometime in the future. Why? she wondered.

"You're English," he observed. It wasn't really a question, he was stating a fact. His voice was deep and had the sugary quality of honey. If he were making love, Stephanie thought, the roughness would disappear and only the golden honey would remain.

"Yes," she acknowledged. She had thought of herself as English for so long that she would never really be anything else, no matter how her birth certificate read.

"You speak French very well."

"Thank you."

It was the only good thing to come out of her brief engagement to Jean-Louis, though even that had seemed doubtful for a time. She had worked very hard to prepare herself to be a fitting wife for an ambitious young diplomat who wanted to get to the very top of the tree. Her family had been appalled by the whole affair, and they had been quite right in the end; Jean-Louis had found her wanting and had moved on elsewhere in search of a wife.

"Where did you learn?" the man pressed her.

"I took a Berlitz course in London."

He picked up the label on her luggage and read it aloud. "Miss Stephanie Ironside." He read further. "You're going to Rouen? Wouldn't it have been easier to have crossed to Dieppe or Le Havre?"

"It's longer on the boat that way," she explained.

The pull of amusement to his lips annoyed her. It was easy for anyone who had never suffered to make light of what she went through from the instant she came on board to the moment she was safely on dry land again.

"I too am going to Rouen," he announced blandly.

She was startled into looking up at him. The sun behind him had presented him with a halo she doubted he deserved. He was incredibly handsome, though not in the usual style, but with an overpowering strength that she liked all the better because it was so completely different from Jean-Louis' pallid good looks which had been as conventional as the clothes he wore. This man had a touch of the devil and was all the better for it in Stephanie's opinion.

"Then why are you going to Boulogne?" she asked him dryly.

He shrugged Gallic shoulders. "My car is there. What do you do in Rouen?"

Stephanie pursed her lips thoughtfully. "I'm an art student," she said at last.

His eyes narrowed as he assessed her answer. "You go to Rouen for that?"

"There's an excellent School of Art there."

"True, but not many English students. Do you know people in Rouen?"

She shook her head. She didn't know anyone in the whole of Normandy, not one single person, and yet, if her mother were to be believed, she was half-Norman herself, and would have been brought up there if her father hadn't been killed in Algeria. She wasn't really entitled to the name Ironside—that had belonged to her stepfather—but her father's name was still too new to her for her to feel that it had anything to do with her.

The coast of France was clearly visible by now. It looked like its name, Cap Gris Nez, the Cape of the Grey Nose. Stephanie shivered. Was that her true land? The one where she would have been born and brought up if her father hadn't been killed? It didn't seem possible. She could never be anything else besides English, and very ordinary English at that.

"You don't admire our Opal Coast?" the man asked her wryly.

She laughed out loud. The French, she knew, could make anything sound like a tourist attraction, but she hadn't heard of the Opal Coast before. It was probably apt though. As far north as England, it probably shared much the same weather, and how else would one describe a sunless, misty day?

"I've never thought about it," she admitted. "I've never thought of France as a place to live before. I've never thought about belonging to anywhere else but the town I grew up."

"And now you're going to belong to Rouen?"

"On a strictly temporary basis."

He said nothing for a long moment, but she was very much aware of his intense look. The silence grew and grew until it became unbearable to her. He looked at her as if he recognised her, and she felt very much the same about him, and yet she knew she didn't know him. He was too attractive for his own good—and for hers!

"Aren't you going to welcome me to France?" she challenged him.

"Indeed," he assured her. "How would you like me to welcome you?"

"You could start by telling me your name," she suggested.

He looked amused. "Wouldn't you rather have a romantic, anonymous admirer who is trying to work out a way of persuading you to let him drive you to Rouen?"

Her eyes opened wide. Perhaps she looked better than she felt, but she doubted it. She began to wonder why he had scraped up an acquaintance with her. Had he recognised her? Surely not! That was her guilty conscience speaking. Her mother had been horrified that she should go to France, to Normandy, without telling her relatives there that she was coming. They had argued about it at length. In vain her mother had pointed out that her father's family would want to get to know her. How could they, when she had only just learned of their existence? What interest had any of them shown in *her* existence so far?

"Perhaps I don't find you very romantic," she remarked.

"When one is suffering from *mal de mer,* nothing is romantic," he agreed. "You'll feel quite differently once we're on our way to Rouen!"

"I doubt it. I haven't a romantic nature."

"No?" His dark eyes laughed at her. "I think you may surprise yourself, mademoiselle. Why else would you come to France?"

She was disappointed in him—and herself, for giving him that impression.

"Not for that!" she stated.

Perhaps he was more astute than she had allowed for after all. He gave her another wry smile.

"One bad experience isn't the whole of life. Ah, Boulogne at last! There goes the announcement that drivers are to return to their cars. Foot passengers are not only the last to get on, but the last to get off, it seems."

This would be the moment to escape if she wanted to, she told herself. The man, as sure of himself as ever, strolled over to the side of the ferry and watched the activity down below as they slipped into the harbour and into their final mooring. He simply didn't believe that she would walk away from him, and that piqued her curiosity. Perhaps he didn't care whether she did or not.

She joined him at the rail. "Are you really going to Rouen?" she asked him. "My name is Stephanie Ironside, by the way."

"Very English," he commented. "Wasn't that the name given to Cromwell's troops in your civil war?"

"The name is older than that," she retorted, somewhat huffily. "I'm a Royalist. They may have been wrong about most things, but they were magnificently romantic, don't you think?"

His eyes crinkled at the corners, betraying his amusement. "It's one view of history. And, yes, I am really going to Rouen, and on beyond."

She fought with herself, trying to make up her mind whether to accept his offer of a lift or not. She glanced sideways at him, noting again his hip-hugging white trousers and the well-developed muscles his shirt did little to conceal. Would he expect a payment she was unwilling to give? She thought it quite likely and wondered why she should still be hesitating. Had her engagement to Jean-Louis taught her nothing?

"It's an awkward journey to Rouen from here," she mused aloud.

"Which is why you're coming with me? Cheer up, Mademoiselle Stephanie, I won't bite!"

"I am booked into a hotel for the night—"

"In Rouen?"

"Well, of course, in Rouen! The School of Art said they'd find me some lodgings, but the term hasn't begun yet. I thought I'd take a look round on my own first."

He smiled slowly. "Then you've nothing to worry about—not today. I'll deliver you to your hotel, I promise. Tomorrow I may suggest another plan to you, but today you'll be as safe with me as if I were your brother. Satisfied?"

She should have been delighted. She was not. When he pulled at the corners of his mouth to stop himself from laughing she couldn't help noticing how firm his lips were. She wondered what it would be like to be kissed by him, and then, startled by her own thoughts, she reddened and turned hastily away.

"I'd better fetch my luggage," she said from the back of her throat. Another moment and he would have guessed what she was thinking. Perhaps she really was getting over Jean-Louis' defection at last. She couldn't ever remember wondering what it was like to be kissed by him! Her whole romance with Jean-Louis had crept up on her when she'd been looking the other way. It had been such a suitable match for her, a ready-made marriage she would have been ungrateful to have refused. Come to think of it, she hadn't much liked it when Jean-Louis had first kissed her, and that was an even more disturbing thought. She had no doubts that she'd more than like it if this man were to kiss her!

He took her heavy case from her, ignoring her protests, and strode off down the companionway to the lower deck, where people were already gathered to flood off the ferry and make their endless way along the newly built walk that took them into the centre of the town.

"Monsieur!" she called after him, struggling to keep up.

He paused and waited for her. "You'd better call me Pierre."

"Pierre what?"

But he was already striding away from her, the covered walk swaying beneath them. Stephanie would have preferred the open air and the drizzle that was now descending on the streets of the fishing port.

Pierre, she muttered under her breath. She had to admit it was apt. He was like a rock all right, as hard and unyielding as the hardest stone on earth. She made a face at his back. What was all the mystery about his name anyway? Who cared what he was called?

He found his car with unerring ease, transferring their luggage into the hatchback rear with the grace of one accustomed to dealing with heavy weights. Only then did he look round to confirm that she had sprinted after him and hadn't got lost along the way.

"If you wore more sensible shoes—"

She exploded with rage. "What's wrong with my shoes?" She lifted her trouser legs to display them more fully. She thought they *were* pretty sensible herself. Perhaps the heels were rather high for travelling in, but she liked high heels.

"Very nice!" Pierre murmured, noting her flushed, angry face with interest. "Let's go and get something to eat and then we can be off."

She put up with his hand on her elbow only because she didn't know where they were going and he did—or she hoped he did, because he was going along ways she had never ventured down before, culminating in what looked like a private opening but where, sure enough, there proved to be a modest-looking restaurant which was crowded out, despite the poverty of its decor, and was therefore probably one of the best in town. To Stephanie's surprise, they were seated immediately, crowding in on the other patrons who amiably moved up a few inches to give them access.

"Most English people like our mussels," Pierre hazarded. "Will that do for you as a starter?"

"It'll probably do for the whole meal!"

He shook his head. "We'll have lamb chops and flageolet beans to follow," he decided. He gave the order, choosing a bottle of wine to go with the meal and then sat back satisfied.

"Do you come here often?" Stephanie asked him.

"I don't come to Boulogne very often. How about you?"

"Once in a while."

He nodded. "I was wondering what inspired you to perfect your French. Not many foreigners take the trouble, particularly as English is the more universal language nowadays."

Stephanie hesitated. But, after all, what harm was there in telling him? "I was engaged to a Frenchman. It was important to his job that I should speak French well."

"What happened?"

"Jean-Louis is going to marry someone else. Someone who will be of far more help to him in his career than I could have been."

Pierre put his head on one side, considering her. "You sound bitter."

She looked down at the bowl of black-shelled mussels in onion soup that had been placed in front of her. "My pride was hurt," she said simply. "Jean-Louis had been the major achievement of my life until his defection."

"Did your parents share your opinion?"

"My mother is a great Francophile."

"And your father?"

She sighed. "He died shortly afterwards. He didn't care for Jean-Louis as a matter-of-fact. He thought he was too charming to be true."

"And you?"

She smiled a weary smile. "I was willing to be charmed."

"You weren't in love with him?"

"I thought I was—not that it's any of your business. I thought I was fathoms deep in love with him, but I wasn't. He surrounded me with a fog of romantic illusions I'd have been a great deal better off without. It shan't happen again!"

"I see. The romantic approach is the wrong one to take with you?"

She nodded an affirmative. "I've done with romance."

"And love?"

"That's different," she stated. "Love is real; romance is not."

His dark eyes sparkled. "It's not impossible to combine the two, *chérie*. One day I shall show you how."

That was something that needed firmly nipping in the bud, she thought. Just because she'd accepted his offer of a lift to Rouen didn't mean that she wanted to know him better, let alone give him ideas that she might be available for anything else he had in mind.

"On that day I'll be working. If I'm ever going to earn my living by my own efforts, work is going to have to be my top priority in the next few months!"

He transferred a morsel to his mouth thoughtfully. "How have you earned a living so far?"

She leaned forward, her green eyes sparking as they met his. "What do you do for a living?" she countered.

"I'm an historian. At the moment I'm engaged in a biography of Guillaume le Conquérant—"

It was a moment before the name came through to her as William the Conqueror, *England's* William the Conqueror! It was a moment longer before she conceded to herself that before he had been England's he had been Normandy's William the Bastard, William the Norseman, whose people had managed to conquer a great deal of Europe one way and another.

"Is that what you were doing in England?" she enquired.

"Not this time. I was in England on a personal mission at the request of the one member of my family who means anything to me. She is a very distant relation of mine, though we share the same surname. When my own parents died, she and her husband took me in and brought me up as their own son. You'll like her, *petite*, when I take you to see her."

It wouldn't have been polite to say she had no intention of meeting anyone to do with him once he had dropped her off at Rouen. He was only being friendly, she decided. He probably still felt sorry for her, as he would for anyone who managed to feel seasick on a Channel ferry. *Why wouldn't he tell her his name?*

The debris of shells from the mussels were taken away and a dish of small light green beans topped with the lamb cutlets were brought in their place. Stephanie fell to with a will, thoroughly enjoying her meal. The beans tasted heavily of garlic, always a favourite with her, and she was glad he was eating it too, though she didn't mean to get any closer to him than they were now. She squinted across the table at him.

"Are you always this nice to damsels in distress?" she asked him.

"There's a first time for everything."

She digested that in silence. "Why me?" she said at last.

"I liked the cut of your jib."

Oh yes? She conjured up a mental picture of herself crouched over the rails, her hair in rat-tails and the rest of her not much more attractive.

"Are you sure you didn't mistake me for a member of the *jeunesse dorée?*" she taunted him.

"Not for a moment. What did your shirt cost? Seven pounds-odd? And your cords not much more? The whole rig, bag included, didn't cost you much more than fifty pounds. Our golden youth spend more than that on eating breakfast after a late party."

"Oh." She was nonplussed.

The lazy lids of his eyes almost hid them from her. "I thought it'd be nice to have you around in case I felt like a kiss later on, my dear Stephanie. Is that what you want to hear?"

"Certainly not!"

"Then, if you don't want anything else, we'd better be on our way." He tossed a few bills onto the table in front of him and stood up, releasing her from her prison behind the cheap wooden table. "We'll stop for coffee along the road, okay?"

"It's fine with me," she agreed. She stood up also, swinging the strap of her bag up onto her shoulder. "I'd sooner pay for my own meal though."

He spread his hands in a Gallic gesture. "We'll argue about that on the way. If you're really an art student you'll need every franc you have just to live, or do you have private means?"

"Not so you'd notice!" she said, and crossed her fingers behind her back. It wasn't a complete lie because now that she knew about her true parentage she didn't feel entitled to accept any more help from her stepfather. He had been more than generous in the past, but now it was up to her to provide for herself. She was determined on it.

Stephanie was almost asleep when they came into Rouen. Pierre found a parking place near the cathedral and shook her awake.

"Recognise where you are?" he smiled at her.

She looked sleepily about her. It was unbelievably familiar, and yet quite different. This was the other half of her heritage, and also the other half of the English heritage. There were the black and white buildings so familiar in parts of England, and yet here they were not black and white—the wooden frames had been painted brown, and the patterns were slightly different, as they had always varied from district to district. The same could be said for the polite architecture. The cathedral was very like its counterparts sprinkled throughout England, and yet it also had its differences; the design Flamboyant rather than Gothic, though the west front could have been a handbook of the latter style.

"Is this Rouen?" she asked, entranced.

"This is Rouen," he confirmed. "You said you were booked into a hotel here."

"Yes, I am."

She stirred and searched in her handbag for the address of the hotel, handing it over to him. His eyebrows rose slightly when he saw her mother's neat writing, and she wondered if it were terribly expensive or had something else wrong with it.

"Mother used to stay there," she defended her choice. "She spent her first honeymoon there."

His eyes narrowed. "Before she married your father?"

How to answer that? Stephanie floundered in silence before compromising by saying, "She spent her second honeymoon on a cruise in the Far East."

"Very romantic," he commented.

"I expect the first one was too," Stephanie pointed out, sounding a bit wistful. "It's the man who makes the honeymoon, not the place."

He looked at her sharply, waiting for her to say something more, but she had nothing more to say. If he knew her mother had been married to a Frenchman, a Norman, he might be even more doubtful about her stated reason for coming to Rouen.

"Oh well," he said at last, "we'd better get you checked in." He took her suitcase out of the back of the car and then helped her out onto the street. "Down there is the rue du Gros Horloge. Under the clock is a café that spills out over the street. That's where I'll meet you tomorrow."

She shook her head. "I'll be busy tomorrow."

"With me," he insisted with a quiet certainty that set her heart knocking against her ribs as if she were afraid of him.

"You don't understand—" she began.

"Indeed I do, *petite*. You thought I'd drive you here

and then go about my own business and that you'd never see me again, but it isn't going to be like that."

Her green eyes flashed. "No?"

"No. We're going to get to know each other a great deal better in every way. Now that you've dried out I can see you're a very pretty girl, too pretty to be left to her own devices in a strange city. We Normans are a very hospitable people. Tante Janine will want to meet you as soon as I've told her about you, and I—I have plans for you too, but it's too early for me to tell you about them now—"

"What plans?" she demanded.

He sighed an elaborate sigh. "I'll meet you under the clock at eleven o'clock tomorrow morning. Maybe I'll tell you then."

"You'll tell me now, or I won't be there!"

"Very well." He took in her indignant face and the pugnacious set to her shoulders. "It's nothing very bad, *ma chère* Stephanie." A muscle twitched in his cheek and he smiled despite himself, his dark eyes catching fire from the source of his private amusement. "First I shall take you home with me, then I'll show you a little of Normandy, then I'll kiss you and then, when we know each other a little better, I'll take you to bed and teach you that love and romance are both best spoken in the French language."

Her mouth fell open at his audacity. "You'll do nothing of the sort!" she denied haughtily.

He picked up her suitcase and gestured for her to precede him down a narrow street, now used by pedestrians.

"I shouldn't bet on it, *petite*," he said. "I'm a very determined man."

"Are you? Are you indeed? And what do you think I am?"

His eyes laughed at her, bringing the hot colour flying up into her cheeks. "I think you're beautiful," he said softly, "and a little shy. But you needn't worry, I'll look after you!"

"You won't get the opportunity!" she assured him. But somehow she herself wasn't at all convinced of that. She had the most horrid feeling that she was going to see a great deal more of Pierre, whether she liked it or not, and she wasn't altogether sorry. On the contrary, she thought he might be dangerous, he might even make her disastrously unhappy, but he'd never bore her to death as Jean-Louis frequently had done. She felt more alive than she had for ages. She felt—she felt like someone on the verge of a great discovery. And that was the most dangerous thing of all.

Chapter Two

The rue du Gros Horloge drew her like a magnet. For
an hour she resisted the temptation to take Pierre at
his word and wait for him in the café under the clock,
but by a few minutes to eleven she would have been
glad of anyone's company, or at least that was what
she was telling herself. She saw him from a long way
off. Now was the time to melt away in the crowds and
pretend, both to herself and him, that she hadn't been
intrigued by his invitation, not even for a minute.

"Stephanie!"

She sat forward in her chair, her eyes on the table in
front of her, in two minds as to whether she would
make a bolt for it after all. The practicalities, however
were against her. She had ordered a cup of coffee and
had not yet paid for it. True, she could have come
back later and made some sort of explanation as to

why she had run away earlier, but her spirits failed her at the mere thought.

"Good morning," she grunted in English.

Pierre stood in front of her, in a navy-blue shirt this time, a pleasant smile breaking up the rather stern lines of his face.

"Drink your coffee, *ma petite*. I'll order one for myself. We have plenty of time. Perhaps you'd like a sandwich, or a *croque-monsieur*? Who knows when you'll get another meal?"

"I do," she informed him loftily. "I shall eat at lunchtime. I've seen a nice little restaurant—"

"You won't be in Rouen at lunchtime."

She stared at him, bristling with indignation. "No?"

"No."

"That's what you think! I'm certainly not going anywhere with you!"

"Don't be ungrateful," he bade her lovingly. "I've arranged a whole programme for your entertainment, to show off my country to you, and to introduce you to my people, and you say you won't come?" His warm laughter was as disbelieving as his tone of voice. "You'll come, Stephanie. Why else are you sitting here in this café, waiting for me?"

"I and half the world are here," she observed sourly. "I came to see the clock like everyone else!"

It was an interesting clock, she reassured herself, and everyone in Rouen did come to see it sooner or later. There were two faces to the clock, each telling the time with a single hand, as well as the day of the week and the phases of the moon. Almost next door were houses dating back to the fourteenth and fifteenth centuries, which had been renovated recently and turned into cafés or the like.

Stephanie studied the clockhouse with an interest she was far from feeling. She noted the steep, man-sarded roof and the arms of Rouen, her eyes dropping down to the relief of the Good Shepherd amongst his flock.

"How was the hotel?" he asked her.

"Charming," she answered.

"Have you paid your bill?"

Her eyebrows rose. "Is that anything to do with you?"

"I think so. You are coming with me, aren't you?"

"That depends on where we're going." Now, why on earth had she said that? If she wasn't careful she would get herself so deeply involved with this man that there would be no way out. She ought to have said goodbye the evening before, and meant goodbye, no matter how attractive he was.

"I'm taking you home."

The words had a double-meaning for her that he couldn't possibly have intended. She supposed that her father's home was hers, even though she knew so little about him. It was strange to think that had he lived she would have been brought up in this country, and not in her mother's. She wondered what kind of a man her father had been. It was unlikely that he would have been one half as wealthy or successful as her stepfather! As far as she knew he had been doing his national service in the French Army when he had been killed. It didn't sound as if he'd had a big share in this world's goods. If he had, he certainly hadn't left anything much to his young widow.

"Home is in England," she said aloud.

The timbered houses around them mocked her. Half your roots are here, they seemed to say. She clenched her fists and sniffed. Not if she could help it, they weren't!

"You haven't seen where I'm taking you yet," he remarked, amused.

She sniffed again. "I'm not going anywhere with you unless I know a great deal more about you than I do now," she informed him in carefully modulated tones. She didn't want to sound unsure, or anxious, or anything other than supremely confident that she could look after herself.

"Tante Janine will tell you all you need to know. I told her you're coming last night. She was annoyed with me for letting you spend a night in Rouen by yourself. A *jeune fille, bien élevée,* such as yourself, might have been frightened without an escort close at hand, she said. Tante Janine is old-fashioned in her ideas, as you'll find out."

It all sounded very respectable. She would have taken it at face value if he hadn't looked so much like a handsome pirate. She knew better nowadays than to trust handsome men. Jean-Louis had been handsome in his way—and just as inclined to ride roughshod over her opinions and plans. Honesty made her admit that that had been partly her own fault. She had laid herself flat to please him, until she had hardly been a person in her own right at all. She had gone to concerts he had chosen, had read the books he had told her to read, and had kept only those of her friends he was prepared to tolerate, which had been few. The best part of their parting was that it had been such bliss to be herself again, with her own friends and interests, and nobody to answer to but herself.

"I'm not sure I want to meet your tante Janine," she said.

"She wants to meet you."

"Why?" Stephanie turned her emerald green eyes fully onto him, noting with satisfaction the sudden tightening of his features. He thought her attractive too! Perhaps she wasn't quite so much at a disadvantage with him as she had thought.

He shrugged his shoulders. "Let's go! Is your luggage at the hotel?"

There was a mystery here she had to solve, wise or not. She nodded as she stood up. She had dressed very carefully that morning, and she was pleased by the effect she was having on him now. She had brushed her honey-coloured hair until it shone, and her dress was exactly the same shade as her eyes and showed her figure off to perfection. She was *glad* she was going with him!

"You lead the way and I'll follow," she said, admiring the ease with which he swung his way through the crowd, whistling under his breath. She had a marvelous view of his strong back, the way his hair curled into the collar of his navy shirt, and the springy step with which he walked, carrying him further away from her at every pace.

Stephanie pursed her lips together and refused to hurry after him. Instead she turned her attention to the cathedral, ostentatiously consulting the guidebook as she walked along. She read all about the Butter Tower, paid for by those citizens who couldn't bring themselves to give up butter for Lent and had preferred to pay for their indulgence in cash instead.

Pierre was waiting for her as she crossed the busy main road at the edge of the area marked off for pedestrians. He was watching her approach in such an obvious way that she could feel her pulse hammering in her throat in response. It was obvious that he was trying to make her feel self-conscious—but she wasn't about to let him know that he was succeeding. He was conceited enough without her adding her mite to his arrogant dealings with her sex. Still, she couldn't quite quench the gush of pleasure it gave her to look at him and to know that his attention, for the moment, was fixed on her.

"I've parked the car round the back," Pierre told her when she at last caught up with him. "Have you seen the Aître Saint-Maclou yet?"

She was cautious. "Should I have?"

"I'd have thought it would have been your first port of call."

"It's the Fine Arts School?"

"Right," he drawled.

Well, she had been going there today. She might have gone that very morning if she hadn't been more tempted to meet him in the rue du Gros Horloge instead.

"I have plenty of time," she defended herself. "I don't have to be there for another week."

"You can go and look at it now if you like," he offered, "I'll fetch your luggage from the hotel."

"What was it before it became the Fine Arts School?"

"A charnel house. You'll find plenty of reminders of its past inside."

They walked together down the rue Saint-Romain with its memories of Joan of Arc. It was there that she was sentenced to death, and it was along that road that she was dragged by the English on the way to her place of execution.

Pierre left her on her own in the tiny square in front of the parish church of Saint-Maclou. "You go through there," he pointed the way out to her. "I'll come for you in fifteen minutes."

That didn't give her long to make her acquaintance with the building that housed the school to which she had gained entry. The old parish cemetery was rewarding however, and she passed a cursory glance around the ancient courtyard, open to the skies, feeling again the sorrow that came to her whenever she visited provincial France. The French saw nothing wrong in allowing old timbers to moulder rather than take the trouble to cover them with an occasional coat of preservative, or whole walls to collapse rather than carry out a few repairs when they started to sag.

Three of the surrounding galleries had been built in 1527, but there was little to choose between them and the fourth, the southern gallery, which had been erected a century later. All the transoms were decorated with funerary attributes such as spades and skulls, and the pillars which supported these heavy beams still bore the remains of a grim dance of death.

Stephanie shivered at one particularly graphic representation. The old, silvered timbers were crumbling away, but the skeleton could still be seen, grinning teeth well to the fore. She wondered if the past's obsession with death had made it easier to accept than it was nowadays in a more sanitised age, when mouldering corpses were kept carefully out of sight and mind, preferably never to be referred to at all. It was a strange place to house a school. She hoped she was going to like it—if she ever got there.

She was too early for Pierre to be waiting for her. She crossed the road and ran down the short distance of the rue Saint-Romain that took her to the hotel where she had spent the night. It had been a good choice of her mother's, pretty and comfortable, with its little courtyard, bright with flowers, over which her room had looked. Their scent came in through the window she had managed to force open, despite the disapproval of the maid who had brought her breakfast up to her.

Pierre looked up as she entered, a smile of welcome breaking across his face. She hesitated in the doorway, astonished by how dear he seemed, how familiar, almost necessary to her well-being, and yet she knew nothing about him, not even his real name.

"There's a difficulty with your luggage," he said.

The proprietress looked up from her desk. "I wasn't prepared to release your suitcase to just anybody, mademoiselle. You might not have wished to accompany this young man. If you remember, you said you might be requiring your room for a further night?"

"Of course," Stephanie smoothed her down. "How kind of you to guard my things so well for me, but it's quite all right. I'm going on a visit to Pierre's aunt, Madame—"

She searched for a name in her mind, her eyes bright with laughter as she watched Pierre seeking a way out of the trap she had laid for him.

"She lives in one of the old manor houses beyond Lisieux," he said.

The proprietress was impressed. "I hope you have a happy stay, mademoiselle."

"I'm sure I shall," Stephanie answered.

It was the first she'd heard of a manor house. She hadn't thought there were any left in France. England was the place that was famous for its country houses and their landed gentry and all that, not France! But perhaps this was another respect in which Normandy had kept her own heritage, another link with the daughtercountry across the Channel.

"Tell me more about this house of your aunt's," she said as they left the hotel.

"It's more an old farmhouse. Normandy is famous for her dairy products and cider."

"I don't think much of the cider."

"What about the cheeses?"

She could find no fault with the cheese, remembering that Camembert was one of them. She shrugged her shoulders. "I've seen old houses before," she insisted doggedly.

"You'll find this one rather special all the same."

She was determined to do nothing of the sort. She wondered why she had agreed to go with him. She must be mad! Worse than mad, because she was old enough to know better than to go chasing after cheap thrills like any other will-o'-the-wisp. Jean-Louis should have taught her that!

The right bank is as important to Rouen as the left

bank is to Paris. Stephanie fastened her seat belt and tried to still the excitement that danced through her veins at the thought of the adventure before her. They crossed the Guillaume le Conquérant Bridge with her still trying to reason herself into a more sober and safer mood. It was pleasant to be able to leave the driving to someone who knew exactly where he was going. She glanced sideways at Pierre from beneath her lashes. The sight of him gave her a start. She longed to reach out a hand and touch him, to study the geography of his body as she might a scene she was going to paint. Perhaps he would sit for a portrait? She chewed thoughtfully on her lower lip, wondering if she had the skill to make her hand do what her mind saw so clearly, a very masculine face with clear-cut lines, heavily lidded eyes, and a mouth that would have made any woman want to know what it would be like to be kissed by him.

She looked down at her hands and was annoyed to find they were shaking. She knotted her fingers together to keep them still and looked determinedly out of the window. She felt hollow inside and a fool besides. Jean-Louis had never made her feel like this, but then Jean-Louis had been a nonentity beside this unknown Pierre.

"If we're going through Lisieux, I'd like to stop and see Saint Thérèse's Carmel and the house where her family lived," she announced to break the silence between them.

"Some other time," he replied smoothly. "Today, I want to get you to Tante Janine's in time to prepare for her birthday dinner." His glance made her feel like a mouse about to be eaten by a marauding cat. "You're part of my birthday present to her," he added. "It's a pity I can't wrap you in a pretty paper and tie a velvet bow round you, though she might not enjoy unwrapping you as much as I would."

Stephanie drew herself up, holding her head high. She wasn't going to rise to such easy bait, she told herself.

"And who is this Tante Janine of yours?" she asked icily.

He cast her another glance. "Don't you know? You really don't know?"

"I shouldn't ask if I did!"

"Her name is Janine Anders," he said gently.

Stephanie started. It had to be a coincidence, but what a coincidence! She swallowed to give herself time to get over the shock.

"What's that to me?" she demanded.

"She had a son named Lucien Anders. He was killed in Algeria when he was still almost a boy. On his last leave in France he had married an English girl who disappeared shortly after his death. Later on, she would write an occasional letter to Tante Janine telling her about the little girl who had been born some weeks after her father had died, enclosing photographs, but never an address to which Tante Janine could have written."

Stephanie gave in to the shock he had dealt her. "She's my grandmother?" she breathed.

"I believe she is."

"Then it wasn't chance that made you take the ferry to Boulogne? You were looking for me?"

"Your mother had written a few days before, informing us you were on your way to Rouen and that she'd told you about your real father's family. She wasn't sure if you'd visit your grandmother or not. She said it had come as a shock to you to discover that her late husband wasn't your father and, coming so soon after the break up of your engagement to Jean-Louis, she was afraid you were rather off the French and hadn't taken kindly to the idea of being half-French yourself." He reached into the pocket of the car and drew out a photograph, tossing it onto her lap. "I recognised you from this!"

Stephanie studied the photograph in silence. It had been taken on the day she had announced her engagement to Jean-Louis Louvain. She had dressed up specially for it, she remembered, anxious to please Jean-Louis. She thought now that all she had done was to make herself look ridiculous. She felt years older than her former self, and she thought she looked it too. Her only comfort was that Jean-Louis looked equally ridiculous, yet she hadn't thought so at the time. She'd admired his three-piece suit and his snowy white shirt with its stiff white collar. She'd thought he looked every inch an important diplomat. Now, she thought he looked as much of a stuffed shirt as his clothes were old-fashioned.

"I'm not flattered," she remarked aloud.

Pierre smiled broadly. "I was glad to see you with your hair down on the boat. I might have been afraid of that young woman."

"What about him?"

He shook his head. "He lacks your style," he said.

Stephanie's breath caught on a laugh. "I was trying

so hard to be the sort of person I thought he wanted me to be. What a waste of time!"

"Forget him," Pierre advised.

"You don't understand," she wailed. "I thought I was in love with him!"

"That had to be a mistake," he agreed with a straight face. "It wouldn't have happened if you'd had someone else to compare him with. Next time you think you're in love, you'll be warned. You couldn't have lived the rest of your life with him!"

She pushed the photograph away from her. "At least I learned to speak French properly," she said.

"Then you lost nothing?"

She blushed, unsure that she'd understood his meaning. "No, I lost nothing," she agreed, "only in my estimation of myself. Neither Mother nor Father liked him much."

"You'll like your grandmother," he told her.

She was rather less sure. Talking about Jean-Louis had revived all the reservations she had ever held about the French race. They didn't even look at history the same way, never telling their children about the famous battles of Agincourt and Crécy, but only of the battles *they* had won.

"We're coming in to Lisieux," Pierre said suddenly. "We haven't far to go now."

It started to rain in Lisieux, clearing the streets in an instant and making it difficult to see where they were going. Stephanie caught a glimpse of the basilica that had been built to meet the needs of the thousands who had made the pilgrimage to the saint, who had incomprehensibly been nicknamed the Little Flower. It sounded better in French and probably matched the

Victorian, bourgeois life into which the saint had been born, but she had always been more interesting than her first, sentimental admirers had made her out to be.

Shortly after Lisieux they turned off into a narrow country lane and the rain stopped. Lowering grey skies hovered over fields full of the brown and white Normandy cows, but they soon cleared away and a watery sun reappeared to remind them it was summer. Pierre slowed the car, bringing it to a gentle stop just as a sunbeam broke through the gloomy clouds.

"If you look straight ahead you can see Tante Janine's house over there. Are you glad you came?"

Stephanie said nothing. She could not. It wasn't at all what she had expected. She'd thought it would be a farmhouse like any of a thousand others. Perhaps quite a large farmhouse, since he had referred to it as a manor, but this was like none other she had ever seen. It was a moated manor of immense charm, beautiful and mellow, with a dreamlike quality that made her wonder if it were real or if some wizard had conjured it up out of some French story book just to reconcile her to her true birthright.

"It's magnificent!" she murmured.

"You get the best view of it from here. It's rather less romantic when one has to live in the place," he said with a wry smile. "We've drained the moat on the other side, turning part of it into a duck pond, but the foundations still suffer from the damp. It creeps up the walls and gets into all the rooms no matter what we do. It needs a fortune spending on the place—a fortune which Tante Janine hasn't got."

"That's true of most of France," Stephanie turned

on him. "You're all feckless about your old buildings."

"One doesn't want the taxman to know one has any
money to spend on anything," Pierre said dryly. "No
Frenchman wants to spend more in taxes than the next
man—and mostly they don't."

Stephanie returned her attention to the house in
front of her. It was separated from the road by two
small fields that a man and woman were scything by
hand, lifting the cut grass onto one of the oldest
farmcarts she had ever seen. She watched, fascinated,
as the woman rolled the bales and pitchforked them
up to the man, the sweat pouring off her weathered
face. It must have been done just this way before the
coming of the machinery most people used nowadays.

The man jumped up onto the tractor to move the
cart away from the entrance gate so that Pierre could
get by. Hens squawked and ducks waddled out of the
way as the car swept up to the front door. A dog came
languidly over to greet them, waving his tail in a
dignified welcome. Stephanie jumped out and patted
him on the head, stretching her cramped muscles with
relief. At the same moment the front door opened
and a middle-aged woman emerged to stand with
conscious effect a few feet away from Pierre, who was
still struggling with the luggage.

Stephanie observed her with interest, noting a pair
of beautiful legs, elegantly shod, a black silk dress that
whispered haute couture, and silver hair so well cut
that it was impossible to guess if the wave in it was
natural or not. Her hug for Pierre was warm and full
of mutual laughter. Stephanie felt a wave of jealousy,
not just because she, too, would have liked to have

greeted Pierre that way, but because her family was a peculiarly undemonstrative one who never touched each other if they could help it.

The elder woman turned to Stephanie. "My dear, at last!" she exclaimed.

Rendered shy by the twinkle in the woman's green eyes that were an exact replica of her own, she submitted to a scented embrace with a sense of fatalism that was quite pleasant in its way.

"Grandmère?" she whispered.

"But of course, *ma chère*, whom else?"

And then they were all sharing in the same warm laughter, just as if they'd always known each other. In a curious way, Stephanie felt as though she had come home.

Chapter Three

"*Enfin!* Come inside, *ma petite*. I hope you're prepared for an exhausting evening? Did Pierre tell you that it's my birthday and the whole family is coming to dinner? I'd like to say they were coming to wish me well—but you'll meet them for yourself. They're my husband's family, as they make abundantly clear on every occasion. They ignore Pierre as if he didn't exist, which angers me very much, almost as much as their wish to dispossess me from the home I've known all my married life!"

Stephanie blinked. "You've lost me," she said. "I didn't even know where I was coming when Pierre practically kidnapped me this morning!"

Green eyes snapped with amusement. "What did he tell you?" her grandmother demanded.

"That he was taking me to visit his aunt who brought him up."

"I see. How trusting you must be to have come with him!"

Stephanie blushed. "He made his aunt out to be somebody very special," she excused herself.

"It's true I brought him up, but we are only very distantly related. I was sad and unhappy with the loss of my son, and your grandfather thought it would be something positive for me to do."

Stephanie allowed herself to be swept into the house ahead of her grandmother, bewildered by the swift change in the landmarks of her life. She had thought that while she was in Rouen she might make a few enquiries about her real father's family, that she might even have invited herself to visit them once, but never in her wildest imaginations had she thought she would find herself in such a house as this!

She looked about the room, admiring the linenfold paneling on the walls and the heavy, carved furniture that had probably sat in the same places since the Middle Ages. Through the mullioned, square-paned windows she caught a glimpse of the green leaves of the trees outside, and the pale sunshine filtering through the branches, casting dappled shadows on the water of the moat.

"My grandfather—?" she began.

"I was widowed late last year. I'm sorry you didn't know him, my dear. It would have meant a great deal to both of us to watch you grow up, and to have you to stay from time to time, but we quite understood, of course, that your stepfather wanted you as his own daughter. It was your mother's decision and she had a perfect right to turn you into an Ironside, if that's what she wanted to do."

Stephanie thought of the man she had always known as her father and decided that her mother had had very little choice in the matter. Nigel Ironside wasn't a man you contradicted lightly. Her mother had thought it perfectly proper that she should give in to him in every way, but Stephanie had wondered in these last few years just how she would have coped with his all-embracing generosity. If he had lived, she would have been stifled by his well-meant concern for her security. As it was, they had already had one or two battles royal, with her mother wringing her hands on the sidelines and pleading with Stephanie not to make trouble over things which mattered so little. Only independence had mattered to Stephanie. She had largely decided to be an artist because her stepfather had disapproved of the whole profession and had wanted her to take up shorthand and typing instead. She had gleefully thumbed her nose at him for being so stuffy and had told him exactly what he could do with his safe job. They hadn't spoken to each other for days afterwards, not until he'd finally given way and agreed to pay for the training she had chosen for herself.

Stephanie gave her grandmother an insouciant look. "It takes some getting used to," she said. "The French have always been foreigners. The funny thing is that one never thinks of oneself as a foreigner. British is best and all that. My stepfather was always very hot on things like that."

"If he made your mother happy, surely that was all that was required of him," her grandmother commented.

"I suppose so." He needn't have taken her over quite so thoroughly, Stephanie thought to herself. She felt somehow cheated that she'd been denied her own heritage, however much Nigel Ironside might have despised it. In a way, she supposed her mother was the more to blame for that, but she had never stood against her husband in anything that Stephanie could remember. She hoped she had been happy, but her mother was a secretive person and she wouldn't discuss her marriage with anyone, not even her daughter.

"I like and admire your mother," Janine continued. "She wrote every year sending photos of you. That's how Pierre recognised you."

Stephanie nodded. "What's Pierre's other name?" she asked.

"He's an Anders too. He had no real name of his own and so your grandfather insisted he should become one of us. You have a lot in common, you two, one way and another."

Stephanie was doubtful about that. She was on the point of saying as much when her grandmother went on, "Unfortunately, we couldn't change the blood in his veins, any more than Mr. Ironside could yours. My husband tried to change things before he died, but he had no luck. I have no right to live in my home of the last fifty years unless I obtain the permission of the family heirs. I don't mind that everything should belong to them after I'm dead and gone. Whilst I'm alive, however, I should prefer to remain here and not be shipped off to an old peoples' home near Paris. I don't like cities, and I'm not very fond of other old people."

"I should think not!" Stephanie agreed, shocked.

"Then you'll help me?"

"How can I possibly do that?"

"My dear child, you may dislike discovering yourself to be a despised foreigner, but who else has a better right? You are the daughter of my only child. You, too, are an Anders!"

Stephanie gaped at her. "I can't believe they really mean to turn you out!" she exclaimed.

Janine smiled gently at her thunderstruck expression. "Wait and see, *chérie,* that's all I ask of you, wait and see. They'll all be here for my birthday party tonight and you'll be able to make up your own mind about them. How convenient that Pierre was able to bring you to me today!"

"I didn't have much choice," Stephanie informed her dryly. "Your Pierre is the most overbearing, arrogant man I've ever met! He practically kidnapped me, did he tell you that?"

"Tell me more! If you were so frightened, why didn't you scream for help?"

"I doubt anyone would have heard me from inside his car," Stephanie replied with aplomb.

"One is always so practical at such times!" Janine mocked her. "What a calm nature you must have, *ma chère.* I don't believe you were frightened at all, whatever you may say now."

"Not when I learned that you'd be here to chaperon me. My own grandmother—"

"*Oh là,* my dear, Pierre wouldn't give a flick of his

fingers for my presence if he'd decided on a romantic interlude with you. Give me credit for also knowing when to mind my own business. Why should I spoil your fun?" She laughed delightedly at Stephanie's outraged expression. "How very English you've turned out to be! But not as shy as you'd like me to believe! I think we're going to have an interesting evening, *n'est-ce pas?*, me with my in-laws, and you with Pierre? I look forward to it!"

Stephanie was far from looking forward to it. She looked up as Pierre came in to join them, smoothing her skirt more closely over her knees and hoping that she wasn't blushing at his appearance.

"Well, are you staying?" he asked cheerfully.

"I'm staying for dinner—no strings attached! I'd have come anyway, if you'd told me what it was all about. I don't like seeing people being pushed around, not unless there's a jolly good reason for it. The family may not accept me as an Anders though, have either of you thought of that?"

Pierre bent over and kissed her lightly on the lips, creating a new chaos in Stephanie's carefully ordered emotions. She swallowed, moving jerkily away from him.

"Anyone can see at a glance you're an Anders," he teased her. "You're the spitting image of your grandmother!"

"If you do that again, I'll go back where I came from, and then what'll you do?"

Pierre's answer was to kiss her again, the tip of his tongue warm against her trembling lips. "What will you do? Run away?" he challenged her.

She opened her eyes wide, drawing in her cheeks as she looked at him. "I'll think of something. The English make very resourceful adversaries, and we never, never run away, no matter what the provocation, unless it's to come back and win on ground of our own choosing. So beware!"

He laughed. "At the moment you look very, very French, *ma chère,* and they can never resist a challenge either!"

Stephanie lowered her lids demurely and pretended not to have heard him, but inside she was laughing. She rather hoped her father had been something like Pierre. He was so much more exciting than Nigel Ironside ever could have been.

Stephanie was unimpressed by her new family. They looked more as though they had come to a funeral rather than a birthday party. She had read about such French people, but had never thought to meet them. They were strictly provincial, of the well-corseted and button-lipped variety. That they had known hard times was written on their smooth, grey faces, but that they were naturally frugal, and would have been if they had lived in the lap of luxury, only became apparent as one listened to their conversation.

Stephanie had only brought one dress with her that she considered to be suitable to the occasion. It was a calf-length dress of shiny gold material that had matt basketwork on the sleeves and part of the bodice. She had felt quite outrageously overdressed from the moment she had made her way down the stairs and had found her grandfather's family mustering their forces in the hall below.

At first, she couldn't make out what they were doing, but as she stood there and watched them, she saw they were fixing labels on all the various bits of furniture, each claiming the pieces they wanted for themselves. They were so intent on what they were doing, it was some time before they noticed her. When they did, they glowered suspiciously at her, the elder man turning a bright puce at the sight of her emerald eyes and honey-coloured hair.

"Mademoiselle!" His mouth turned down at the corners as he took in her colourful appearance. "Who invited you here?"

Stephanie smiled at him, holding out her hand. "My grandmother. You must be her brother-in-law?"

"François Anders," he supplied reluctantly. "I suppose you have proof you are who you say you are?"

"Grandmère is satisfied," Stephanie returned gently.

"She would be!" he snorted. "I wouldn't be surprised if that impossible adopted boy of hers put her up to this! We made enquiries—several times—and came to the conclusion she had no granddaughter. The shock of being widowed could have brought on a stroke."

"Yet here I am," Stephanie assured him. "I was brought up with my stepfather's name, which is probably why you couldn't find me."

Her great-uncle's wife stirred restlessly. "Who is this, dear?" she asked her husband. She looked for all the world like a twitching white mouse.

"Says she's Janine's granddaughter. Don't believe a word of it, of course!"

"Of course not, dear."

The younger couple joined the little group in the hall. "I'm your cousin, Gérard," the man introduced himself. "This is my wife Berthe. My father, François, and my mother, Héloïse. You can't blame us for being a bit suspicious, as we didn't know you existed. Heard about you often, but as nobody could ever find you, we jumped to the obvious conclusion. Tante Janine is rather a difficult old lady, I'm afraid. It's obvious to all of us that she needs more care and attention than she's getting here. This house is too much for her for a start. But she won't see it that way. Insists she means to go on living here by herself, which I'm sure you agree is impossible!"

Stephanie shook hands with them one by one. "I am Stephanie Ironside," she supplied.

"Ironside!" Her uncle beamed his satisfaction. "We thought you were claiming to be Guy Anders' daughter."

"I am. My stepfather's name was Ironside. He died recently and it was only then that my mother told me he wasn't my real father. I haven't entirely got used to the idea myself yet."

"Well, well, I'm sure you're a sensible girl," her uncle commended her. "If you've only just met your grandmother—and I'm not yet convinced she is your grandmother—you won't know how her health has deteriorated since my brother's death. A devoted couple! She'll be better off in Paris with people to look after her."

"Maybe," Stephanie said, refusing to commit herself. She found herself looking round for Pierre and curbed herself crossly. What did it matter to her whether he was there or not?

"François always knows best," his wife put in with a nervous twitch. "Janine's style of life—it doesn't suit the kind of people we are. My brother-in-law indulged her shamefully but, when there's no money left, one has to put up with things as they really are." A contemptuous glance from her son reduced her to silence. She and Berthe clung together, their menfolk closing in about Stephanie. *Where was Pierre?*

And then, suddenly, he was there. Stephanie breathed a sigh of relief, telling herself that most of her pleasure at the sight of him was because she was being so hard pressed by her new relations.

Pierre regarded the family with obvious amusement. Where they had before been disapproving, it was easy to see that their dislike for Pierre was something much stronger than that. They were uncomfortable in his presence and they resented the fact. Stephanie thought they would have liked to have despised him, but he wasn't an easy person to despise. He stood nearly a head taller than either of the men, his eyes snapping with some private joke of his own, completely unimpressed by their sense of their own importance.

"Tante Janine welcomes you to her house," he drawled. "Come into the salon and have a drink. She'll be with us in just a minute."

"Janine'll be late for her own funeral," François fumed.

"We only allow ourselves a drink on very special

occasions these days," Héloïse fussed beside him. "All these new taxes! One can hardly afford to live!"

Pierre put a hand beneath her elbow and ushered her into the salon, bending a little towards her to hear what she was saying.

"Even with the new taxes, Tante Janine will want us to keep up all the old traditions," he assured her.

"But can she afford it, Pierre. We can afford nothing these days!"

"I can afford it, even if she can't."

Gérard, who had been standing so close to Stephanie she had anxiously shuffled her toes out of his way, heard this last and rushed forward to have his say, his wife and Stephanie both forgotten for the moment.

"I'm surprised you can afford anything!" he fired off at Pierre. "What are you doing now? Still sponging off your benefactress? She might have been able to keep on living here if it hadn't been for you!"

Pierre went on looking amused. "Look after Berthe," he advised softly. "You nearly knocked her over in the doorway."

"Berthe can look after herself!"

"She probably has to," Pierre agreed readily.

Berthe, the colour of a tomato, came unhappily into the room. She cast her husband an agonised glance, knotting her fingers together in front of her, almost as if she were willing herself to disappear into thin air.

"Berthe is a modern woman who works for her own living," Gérard growled. "She doesn't need any man to look after her."

Stephanie looked from one to the other of her relations, disliking them more than she could say.

"We all have a need for common courtesy," she said slowly and clearly. "Pierre, are you going to get the drinks?"

It was only when she saw her great-uncle's stunned expression that she realised how fully she had assumed the role of substitute hostess. For a minute she was thrown, thinking she might have taken too much on herself, but her dislike for these people stiffened her backbone. If she was an Anders by birth, why shouldn't she behave like one? She couldn't see why this group of nasties should have everything their own way.

Pierre put a brandy into her hand and came and stood beside her. There was a special glass put aside for her grandmother. A picture of the manor house had been cut into its surface, together with her initials and a date.

Stephanie picked it up and examined it. "Another special occasion?" she asked.

Pierre nodded. "That was the day she first came here. Her wedding day."

Stephanie put the glass back on the table. "Her wedding day and her birthday. Fifty-two years is quite a slice out of anyone's life."

"You should've been here for their fiftieth anniversary," Pierre told her. "That was a day and a half."

"*We* weren't invited," Héloise remembered with chagrin. "Janine has always ignored us whenever she could. She forgets that François is just as much an Anders as her husband ever was."

"It wasn't Anders money that bought this place," Pierre murmured. "My uncle did it all on his own."

"Janine was no help to him! The only contribution she made was to bring you into the family!"

"You know," said Pierre, "you really shouldn't speak about things you know nothing about."

"We know what was in Guillaume's will," François retorted angrily. "That's all we need to know. *You* aren't in it because you're not a true Anders. Even Guillaume, besotted as he was, recognised that!"

Pierre raised his glass, contemplating the liquid within. "Sometimes I'm quite glad I'm not an Anders," he mocked them. He shook his head at Stephanie. "Is your heritage what you expected, *petite?*"

She laughed, turning away. "You forget, I'm an Englishwoman through and through, no matter what my father was. I'm more Ironside than Anders."

"Tante Janine was a Devaligne. I can remember when her hair, too, was the colour of champagne—"

"The Devalignes had nothing!"

Pierre lifted a quizzical brow. "Are you sure?"

There was a moment's silence. The Anders family shuffled their feet and glared at Pierre. Stephanie heard a slight rustle outside and then her grandmother appeared, her back as straight as a ramrod, and her black silk dress an artistic triumph. She looked every inch a grande dame of the old school, and Stephanie was proud of her. Emerald eyes met emerald eyes briefly. It was like looking at oneself in the glass— what she would be like in another fifty years. She could do a lot worse, Stephanie thought.

Somehow the rest of the family looked smaller, with the one exception of Pierre as he went to greet his aunt. They made everyone else in the room look mean and shabby. Stephanie remembered how she had felt, coming down the stairs towards them, like a bird of paradise lost amongst a group of squabbling sparrows. Her grandmother and Pierre walked with the pride of peacocks. Even she felt as though she had to stand straighter and hold her head up higher as she watched them.

"You're late!" François broke the silence.

"As always," Janine answered him. "I hope I'm worth waiting for?"

"You're looking well," he muttered, the words wrung out of him.

Janine eyed him expectantly for a moment, shrugged elegant shoulders and turned away. "Is that my drink?" she asked, seizing her own special glass. "How this does bring back memories!"

"Bon anniversaire, Tante!" Pierre toasted her.

The others lifted their glasses. "Grandmère," Stephanie added her good wishes.

Her grandmother's eyes filled with sudden tears. "Ah, Stephanie, how much pleasure it gives me to have you here to celebrate my birthday. Pierre won't mind my saying there has always been something lacking since Guy—enough of that! You weren't even born then, and now here you are completing the circle. Have you met all the members of your grandfather's family?"

"You'll have to prove she is whom you say she is," Gérard said truculently. "You haven't been yourself recently, Tante Janine, not since you've been on your own. Anyone could take advantage of your good nature. You'd do well to be advised by Papa. *He* has your interests at heart."

"And Pierre hasn't?"

"Pierre isn't family."

The old lady drew herself up. "He's my family."

Gérard snorted. "What has he ever done for you except give you a lot of unrealistic ideas of how and where you should live? You're getting old, and you'll never be able to go on living in this house by yourself. You'll be much more comfortable in Paris."

"I hate Paris."

Gérard warmed to his theme. "Nobody hates Paris, Tante. It's the centre of French civilisation—"

"It's an overgrown concrete jungle!"

Gérard turned to Stephanie. "I told you she's getting senile. Wouldn't you welcome the chance to live in Paris?"

"No," said Stephanie.

Her grandmother crowed in open triumph. "Where do you live, Stephanie? I've often wondered what kind of man your stepfather was. It would amuse me very much to have you tell us all about your life in England at dinner. Shall we go in, everybody? I'll lead the way and then Pierre can give you his arm without splitting himself in two."

Stephanie gasped when she saw the dining room. The long refectory table was set with the finest Sèvres china, and some of the best French glass. There were flowers on the table which set off the snowy white of the linen. If the salon was formal and uncomfortable, in the dining room the French way of life came into its own. It was truly magnificent.

Pierre seated his aunt halfway down the table, taking his place opposite her and signaling Stephanie to sit at his right hand. In England they would have taken the two ends of the table, but this arrangement had its own convenience, especially as everyone else took their places, only to find themselves almost totally excluded from the centre of things.

Janine poured herself a glass of wine. "To my granddaughter, who was lost, and who now is found," she said.

"You can't be sure, Janine," Héloise pleaded with her. "She looks a little like you to be sure, but that doesn't *prove* anything."

"I'm satisfied," Janine assured her. Her eyes looked her granddaughter over. "I'm more than satisfied."

Stephanie gave her back look for look. "Thank you, Grandmère. I'll be satisfied too if I look as beautiful as you do when I'm your age."

The meal progressed from course to course, brought in from the kitchen by a uniformed maid. Stephanie forgot to hold on to her knife and fork the first time round but, as she told herself, she wasn't accustomed to eating in French houses and if her manners were English, well, so was she. At least she brought a healthy appetite to the feast. She had always been led to believe that the French revered their food more than anything else in the world, especially the Normans. The Anders family, however, picked at everything that was put in front of them, making disparaging remarks about everything. This was too expensive, that was unsuitable for elderly people to eat at night, the other was too rich for anyone who suffered from their livers, as apparently they all did, including Berthe, whose ruddy glow of health belied her concern with the intimate details of the workings of her digestive system.

All things come to an end, however, even seemingly interminable meals. The only note of interest for Stephanie was struck when Pierre insisted they should have a pause between the main course and the dessert, and produced a bottle of well-matured Calvados, the apple brandy that was famous throughout the region.

"This is known as the Norman Pause," Pierre told her, filling her glass almost to the brim.

Stephanie took a sip and choked. It was much stronger than she had expected, and she wondered if she were wise to indulge. She needed her wits about her if she were to prove to be an able ally to her grandmother, whose cause was becoming more precious to her by the minute.

It was Pierre who escorted her from the dining room, putting a familiar hand about her waist.

"Now you know what Tante Janine is up against!" he murmured into her ear.

"Why did she invite them?" Stephanie returned.

"The house is entailed. Haven't you realised that?"

"But they couldn't really be so cruel as to turn her out." Her eyes opened wide. "Could they?"

"They've gone to a lot of trouble to find this twilight home in Paris for her to go to. It's inexpensive and she'll be with other people of her own age, or even older—"

"I can imagine," Stephanie cut him off dryly.

Pierre smiled at her with genuine approval. "I knew we could count on you from the first moment I set eyes on you," he said.

Chapter Four

It was more like a funeral than ever as they gathered in the salon for coffee. Stephanie made to free herself from Pierre's restraining hand, but his only response was to tighten his hold on her. It had definitely been a mistake to drink that Calvados; she felt weak at the knees and slightly breathless, as though she'd been running. Pierre's body was as hard as a piece of wood. She couldn't help comparing his firmness with the rather flabby flesh of Jean-Louis. Of course it wasn't the sort of thing that bothered one when one was in love, but she was well along in the process of getting over Jean-Louis' defection, and she was very conscious of the difference between the two men.

François accepted his cup of coffee, looking at it as if it might poison him at any moment.

"We didn't come only to eat, Janine. It's time we

seriously discussed your future. I owe it to my brother's memory to do what I can for you—he would have expected it—and I intend to do exactly that, no matter what difficulties you put in my way."

Janine sipped her own coffee. "Guillaume and I talked about my future before he died—"

"He always indulged you, even when you were being quite unreasonable!" her brother-in-law snorted. "Look at the way he allowed you to take Pierre into your household. *That* must have cost him a pretty penny, one way and another. A boy who had no claim on your affections! Hardly a member of the family, was he?"

"A distant member. He had no one else, François. Would you have had us abandon him?"

"He meant nothing to any of us!"

Janine looked cross for the first time that evening. "He meant, and means, a great deal to me!" she declared valiantly.

"All the better that he can't inherit under the terms of Guillaume's will. I've no doubt at all you'd have soon talked him into allowing you to stay here on your own."

"He has nothing to gain by seeing me in a poky little flat in Paris! Do you mean to live here yourself, François, or are you planning to sell the house and farm, or what?"

"We're thinking of what is best for you. We might keep an item or two of the furniture, no more than that. The money would be put in trust for you, to keep you in comfort for the rest of your days. I'm only doing my duty!"

Janine sighed. "Then you'll be relieved to know that you needn't do anything more for me, any of you. Guillaume knew as well as I did that we had a grandchild living in England. D'you think he'd have left his will as he did if he hadn't been sure of that? I'm sorry to disappoint you, François, but the house is entailed in the *direct* line. It's really nothing to do with you what I choose to do with the rest of my life."

Consternation spread amongst the four Anders. Stephanie could have laughed out loud. She picked at the label one of them had stuck on the carved armoire that graced one corner of the room. She turned instinctively to Pierre, knowing he would share her amusement at their defeat, only to find him staring at her as if he was seeing her for the first time, and not much liking what he saw. The ready colour sprang into her face and she turned away, hating the silent accusation in his eyes.

She was the grandchild! She sank onto the nearest chair and tried to catch her breath, hoping no one else had noticed her complete confusion. Did that mean that the house now belonged to her? If so, what on earth was she to do with it?

She became conscious that everyone was looking at her, the Anders with a mixture of hatred and suspicion, her grandmother as though she had just brought off a significant coup, and Pierre—what did Pierre want from her? She hadn't wanted any of this! She wished she were back in Rouen, or, better still, back in England with nothing more on her mind than carving out a career for herself in the difficult world of art and modern design.

"You can't be absolutely sure that I am your granddaughter!" she burst out. Her grandmother began to laugh. "Can you?" she demanded.

"I think so," Janine said gently.

Stephanie sucked in her breath. "How?"

"It won't be very difficult, *ma chère*. There's your birth certificate, as well as your mother's letters to me over the years."

"I'm an Ironside!" Stephanie maintained doggedly.

"The devil you are!" Pierre retorted. "What would an Ironside have been doing in Rouen on her own?"

Stephanie's eyes spat fire. "We've been through all that! I'm going to the art school there and *nothing* and *nobody* is going to stop me!"

They might have been alone in the room as far as she was concerned. At that moment he was the only person in the world who mattered to her. He took a great deal too much for granted. He had right from the beginning. What did he know about her anyway?

He shrugged his shoulders. "Why bother now? You have what you want here. A whole new family, a house—"

"Ah, so that's it!" Stephanie exclaimed, burning up. "You think I want this house as much as the rest of you seem to! Well, I wouldn't live in it if you paid me to! I wouldn't live in Normandy, in *France!* I don't even like French people. I've been trying to be fair to you, to tell myself that one bad experience doesn't mean that every Frenchman is utterly selfish and out for the main chance, but you and your family are the living proof of it! Let me tell you that in England we don't go round sticking labels on somebody else's furniture just because we think it would look better in our house! We wait for the duck to die before we pluck it! You're impossible, all of you!"

The silence that greeted this tirade was mingled with an almost total incomprehension on the part of her listeners. Too late, she realised she had been yelling at Pierre in English, and that nobody there spoke the language. Except Pierre. He understood all right. He understood only too well. He stood facing her, his legs a little apart, and he threw back his head and laughed at her.

"Do you want me to translate?" he asked her.

"No, thank you."

This time her grandmother joined him in his laughter. *"La pauvre petite,"* she commiserated. "If you so dislike your father's country, why did you choose to come here for your training?"

"I chose Rouen," Stephanie answered through her teeth. "I may not have come here at all. In fact I probably wouldn't have done. My mother was anxious that I should get to know you all, but I thought I owed my father—my stepfather—something too. He brought me up as his own daughter and I loved him as my father. Guy Anders is no more than a name to me. A stranger."

Madame Anders looked sad. "You're right," she acknowledged at last, "we have no claim on you if you don't want to recognise us as a part of your family. No one needs three grandmothers, do they?"

Stephanie's conscience pricked her. Even so, she might not have given in if she hadn't noticed the sudden eagerness in her great-uncle's face. He thinks

I'm going to refuse my inheritance and that he'll get his own way after all, she found herself thinking. Over my dead body.

"I never knew my grandparents on the Ironside side," she said aloud. "My stepfather was much older than my mother, and they were already dead when he married her."

"But you have your mother's parents?"

Stephanie's expression softened. She had spent many happy hours with her maternal grandparents. In many ways she had preferred being with them to being at home. Neither of them had ever objected to getting dirty, or being bossed about in the execution of one of her wilder schemes, and they laughed a lot, which neither of her parents did at home.

"Yes, I love them dearly. It was Grandma who suggested I might call on you while I was in Rouen. She said that Guy Anders was quite another kettle of fish from Jean-Louis."

"Jean-Louis?"

"My ex-fiancé."

"He's the reason Stephanie speaks French so well," Pierre supplied in a dry tone. "She loses her temper in English though. Isn't that interesting?"

The hairs rose on the back of Stephanie's neck. "I haven't begun to lose my temper yet!" she began angrily.

He rolled his eyes heavenwards. "No? Well, I don't think I want to be around when you do. I'm off home, Tante. Everyone knows where they're sleeping, I trust?"

It was one thing to fight with him when he was

there, it was quite another to be left to face her new relations without him.

"Don't you live here?" Stephanie asked him.

"I have my own house about four kilometres away. I keep an eye on Tante Janine's farm from there."

The back of Stephanie's throat felt as unyielding as a piece of wood. Surely she couldn't be afraid of the Anders? What could they do to her, for heaven's sake?

"Is your house a manor like this one too?" she mocked him.

"Come and see for yourself," he invited her.

For an agonised moment she wondered if she would be wise to take him up on the suggestion. Anything was better than having to talk to her gloomy family, she decided. Besides, there was a certain excitement in picking up the challenge he was so blatantly offering her.

"I'll get a wrap," she said.

Both Héloise and Berthe tried to dissuade her. She didn't know Pierre the way they did, they hinted. He had had a reputation with the ladies since the first time it had been their misfortune to meet him. He had charmed Janine, but now it was the younger women who were in danger from him.

Her grandmother, however, made no effort to stop her from going with Pierre, if that was what she wanted. She came to the front door with her, rearranging her wrap more elegantly around her shoulders.

"That Pierre should run away I can forgive, as they've always been so abominably rude to him," she whispered, "but that you should desert me too, *mon enfant,* is too bad of you! I think I shall say I'm tired and in need of my bed."

Stephanie paused uncertainly. "I shan't be gone long—"

"And they can be as rude as they like behind your back? They will be, my dear, they will be, but I shall have the last laugh, knowing that you can thwart their plans any time you choose. *A demain, petite.* Sleep well."

It was odd to kiss this stranger who was her grandmother goodnight, odder still that it should feel so familiar to her, and so right. Even the scent the older woman wore was one she felt she had known all her life. It was light and smelt of roses.

"Good night, Grandmère," she whispered in her turn.

"I'll bring her back safe and sound," Pierre drawled behind her. Janine cupped his chin with a loving hand. "Do you doubt me?" he teased her.

"I think Stephanie is a very attractive girl, *mon fils.* And, if I think so, I'm very well aware of what you're thinking. Try and remember she's my granddaughter."

He grinned. "There's no chance of my forgetting!"

All the same, Stephanie wondered if she'd been wise to go with him as she stepped into his car and the door closed on her. She was very conscious of his male presence as he got in beside her and set the car in motion. As he changed gear, his trousers were tight against his thigh and she hastily looked the other way, annoyed with herself because she still couldn't control the tingling awareness of her body. She wanted to reach out and touch those hard muscles. Moreover, she wanted to caress the strong, tanned column of his neck and feel the warmth of his lips against her own.

"Was my grandfather anything like his brother?" she asked to give herself something else to think about.

Pierre glanced sideways at her. "Can you imagine Tante Janine married to François?"

She laughed, partly in relief at the lightening of the atmosphere between them. "No, I can't. How did he get to be so mean?"

"Mean?" Pierre's smile grew broader. "He would prefer to be called thrifty. My uncle was a shocking spendthrift in his opinion. A house with two, if not three, spare rooms which he enjoyed filling with his friends at weekends. And then there was the money he spent on my upbringing and education. Worse still, he was prepared to accept me as his own, and gave me his name—me, a mere connection of his wife's, who had no possible claim on his charity!"

Stephanie looked puzzled. "What does he want all this money for?"

"Like all misers, he wants to put it in the bank and count it every now and then. Gérard is just like him, except that he doesn't even trust the banks to look after his money. I'm sure he and Berthe keep it in an old sock under their mattress."

Stephanie was disbelieving. "They couldn't!"

"Oh, the French can be very careful of their money. They have a reputation for it. You'll have to be careful that it doesn't come out in you!"

"I hope not! I can't imagine myself sticking labels onto someone else's furniture, no matter what the circumstances!"

He looked amused. "Is that what they were doing?"

"I came down the stairs and there they were, scurrying from one piece to another, arguing as to who should have what. I couldn't believe it!"

He laughed out loud, putting a broad hand on her knee which sent a shock wave through her body that had her more than a little worried.

"They couldn't believe you, either," he told her. "Tante Janine spiked their guns nicely. You arrived just in the nick of time."

"I'm not sure about that yet," Stephanie confessed. "If you'd told me at the beginning—"

"You wouldn't have come, would you? Your grandmother needed your support tonight, not sometime in a couple of months, when you'd have got your courage up to come and visit her. It could have been too late then."

"I still think you behaved in a very high-handed manner," she said coldly. She couldn't afford to relax for an instant in his presence, especially not if he were to touch her again. "My mother should've told me more about my father too. I'm still not sure I've done the right thing."

"You've got time to make up your mind," he reassured her cheerfully.

"Have I?" She wished she could be as sure as he seemed to be. She didn't feel sure of anything, not even of her own feelings. "Fools rush in and all that! Your Tante Janine could buy and sell any one of those Anders if she set her mind on it, so why doesn't she?"

"It could be that you're her chosen instrument, *ma chère.*"

"And you resent that, don't you?" she sighed. "You don't really like me much as a person, do you?"

He swung off the narrow country road, into a rutted, muddy driveway that led up to an ancient wood-framed house that nestled under an ancient apple tree. It was much less pretentious than the house they'd just left, and it had a much friendlier aspect. It felt warm and loved, as if its owners had always been happy there.

"How long have you lived here?" she asked, forgetting what she had been saying earlier.

"It's always been mine. It was all that was left of my parents' estate after they died. Tante Janine was determined it would be kept for me though, and so it was."

Another example of her grandmother's determination? Perhaps. Yet it had been kindly, too, to keep a small boy's home ready for him for when he was old enough to live in it himself.

"You're very fond of her, aren't you?" The words were out before she could stop them.

He grinned. "Jealous?"

"Of course not!" she denied.

He got out of the car and came round to her side to help her alight. "You know something Stephanie Ironside Anders, I think you're a sore loser. You didn't reckon on having any competition for your grandmother's attention, did you? You thought the prodigal would return and the fatted calf would be roasted for you, without you having to do anything to deserve it. Unfortunately for you, Tante Janine and I have been looking out for one another for a good many years now, and I won't see her taken for a ride by anyone. Understood?"

Stephanie was astonished. "Haven't you forgotten that it was you who brought me here in the first place?"

"I hurried up the process. You wouldn't have stayed away though, would you?"

"I may have."

"I doubt it!" He rearranged her wrap around her shoulders, his fingers brushing against her naked flesh. She shivered, unable to prevent herself, and quickly stepped away from him, only to be caught up short and returned to the circle of his arms. "You're like the rest of the Anders, out for what you can get!"

She faced him bravely. "How d'you work that out?"

"Your mother lived here for nearly a year. She probably told you of all the pickings that were going if you played your cards right."

"She told me nothing at all!"

"Nothing? I don't believe you, Stephanie. Why, you weren't in the least surprised when Tante Janine announced that the entail brought the house to you. You were expecting it. You never even changed expression!"

"*What?*"

He gave her a little shake. "I'd hoped for better things from you, but you're up to every trick, aren't you? There's nothing Tante Janine would like better than for us to get together. Is that why you're here now?"

She shook her head. "I'm here now because I was

afraid I might be rude to my grandmother's guests. It had nothing to do with you, and very little to do with her."

He raised an eyebrow. "Nothing?"

"Nothing," she maintained, lifting her chin as she spoke.

He took advantage of her closeness by ducking his head, and his lips met hers in a smacking kiss that knocked her off balance, leaving her no choice but to cling to him if she wanted to keep upright.

"Let me go!" she demanded crossly, pushing away from him.

"Why should I? You kiss as nicely as you lie, *ma petite*. And you enjoy it, so don't pretend about that too."

She was outraged. "I'm going home," she announced. "Please take me back to my grandmother at once!"

"Does it feel like home already?" he taunted her.

She stamped her foot with rage. "If it means getting away from you, call it anything you like!"

He laughed, as amused by her anger as he appeared to be about everything else about her. "You haven't seen my house yet," he reminded her.

"I don't want to!"

He clicked his tongue against his teeth. "That's not the way to get on with your new family," he reproved her. "I prefer you soft and surprised and loving! Come on, and I'll show you around."

She pulled back, but he was stronger than she, towing her after him with the greatest of ease. He paused for an instant to unlock the front door, standing back and pushing her into the darkened house ahead of him. Outside the sun was setting, inside it was already dark, and she had to blink to adjust her eyes to the shadows to see where she was going. It was a very old house, with uneven floors and walls that wandered off at odd angles, the dark beams looking quite menacing in the darkness.

He switched on a light and she swallowed, ashamed of the prickling fear that lingered on the back of her hands.

"Has this always been a farmhouse?" she asked in a voice not quite her own.

"Come, I'll show you the dairy and the old apple-store. The ones at the manor are bigger and better, but these are more than adequate for my purposes."

The dairy was as clean as a new pin, despite its great age. Here too, the walls bulged and the windows were set-in at odd angles, but the equipment was modern and the cheeses stood on a ledge along one of the walls, maturing and gaining in flavour.

"What kind of cheese do you make?" she asked, interested despite herself.

"All the Normandy cheeses. Camembert, Pont l'Evêque, ordinary cream cheeses. It's more of a hobby with me. I sell them at the local markets and to my friends. There are too many rules and regulations these days, unless one wants to do nothing else."

"I like Camembert; Pont l'Evêque I don't know."

"It's older than Camembert," he told her. "It's stronger too. Do you know the story of the Camembert cheese?"

She shook her head. A few minutes ago who would have believed she would be standing beside this man in a dairy, discussing cheeses?

"Camembert is a little village near Vimoutiers. At the end of the eighteenth century, a certain Marie Harel began to make the cheese that made the whole district famous. There's a *stèle* in the village commemorating her, which is rather better than the statue of her which is to be found in the church of Vimoutiers, complete with pitcher and sabots. It lost its head in the bombing during the war. A replacement statue was given by four hundred men and women who work in a cheese factory in Ohio, but that makes her look like Snow White—suitable, in its way, as it shows the difference between a farmhouse and a factory Camembert cheese as nothing else could."

"A pretty girl is many peoples' ideal. Perhaps it sells more cheeses?"

"It may, but it isn't Marie Harel. The cheese they produce isn't Camembert either!" He took out a long, scooped knife from a drawer and dug it into the cheese that was the closest to being ready, picking out the cheese between his fingers and handing it to her. "Try that!" he commanded.

She did so. It was very good. "If I stayed in Normandy for long, I'd soon be as fat as butter!" she exclaimed. "Look at all that cream we had at dinner— and now this!"

He looked her over with appreciation. "Tante Janine won't let you get away now that she's seen you."

Stephanie leaned against one of the sinks, her head on one side. "I think you're the one who's jealous," she said at last. "You're accustomed to having her attention all to yourself, and you don't like sharing with anyone else."

He refused to take her jibe seriously. "Your father

always came first in her affections. I'm used to taking second place."

"The dead aren't much competition to the living!"

His lips twisted into a wry smile. "That's what you think! If you'd asked Nigel Ironside that question you might have got a different answer."

"My mother was a devoted wife!" Stephanie exclaimed.

"Oh, quite. She never mentioned Guy Anders' name, but d'you suppose she forgot him? How could she, when she had you to remind her of him every day? He had green eyes too, and a strong look of your grandmother. Take a look at his portrait sometime, and then tell me your stepfather came first with his wife!"

"I've never even seen a photograph of him," Stephanie denied, frowning. "We were a complete family without him."

Pierre put his hand over hers, imprisoning her with his weight. "You'll find the portrait in Tante Janine's bedroom. I used to look at it a lot, and wonder what he had that I hadn't. Perhaps you'll be able to tell me. You can work the same magic that he worked—even on me. You wouldn't come second best to anyone, would you?"

Puzzled, Stephanie looked deep into his almost black eyes. "I don't believe you would either," she murmured.

"Not with you!" he agreed, and he put his arms right round her and pulled her hard against him. "It's all or nothing with me, so which is it going to be?"

Chapter Five

It was early when Stephanie awoke, slept out, despite the lateness of the hour when she had finally gone to bed. There was no sound that anyone else was stirring, but she was too restless to remain in bed for a minute longer. The sun came pouring in through the window, beckoning her to put on some clothes and explore what she could of her grandmother's house.

She tried to make her mind a blank as she went through her wardrobe, seeking something suitable to wear. It had been a mistake to take the easy way out and to have gone with Pierre last night. She should have stayed where she was and faced up to the Anders family. All she had succeeded in doing was to put off the inevitable—and the cost had been high, to her at least.

To get away from her unwelcome thoughts, she

rushed downstairs and went straight outside. The memory of Pierre's kisses went with her, making her go hot and cold all over. She had been helpless from the first moment he had taken her into his arms. A melting softness had overtaken her and all thoughts of trying to prove to him that she was an independent English woman with a career on her mind, and not a greedy Anders looking for what she could get, had vanished with the first touch of his lips on hers.

She would do better next time! Better still if there was *no* next time. It shouldn't be impossible to make sure that she was never alone with him again. In a day or so she could go thankfully back to Rouen, and take up her life where he had interrupted it, safely an Ironside once again.

Looking about her, Stephanie found she had blundered into what had once been a rose garden. Years of neglect had almost strangled the bushes with weeds, but some of them were still gamely flowering in the midst of the wilderness. It wouldn't take much to restore order to the beds, she thought, and it would give her something to do that would keep her well away from both Pierre and her new relations.

It wasn't long before she detected her mother's hand in the planning of the garden. All her mother's confirmed favourites were there, easily recognised from her present garden where Mrs. Ironside weekly fought the gardener for permission to pick her own flowers for the house. It was strange to think that Mrs. Ironside had once been the Mme. Anders who had designed and planted this typically English kind of garden.

"It hasn't taken you long to take a proprietorial interest in your new home!"

Stephanie started, and tore the side of her finger on a thorn. "Go away!" she said shortly.

Pierre stood on the unkempt path, his hands in his pockets. "You look as though you could do with some help."

"The only help I need is to be told where the compost heap is. Otherwise I can manage quite well by myself."

He looked at her, a frown between his eyes. "Why begin here?" he asked at last.

Stephanie sucked at her finger, managing to squeeze out a tiny droplet of blood. It hardly hurt at all, but such was her annoyance with Pierre for surprising her that she wanted to make as much of it as she could.

"This was my mother's garden, wasn't it?"

The frown increased. "Did she tell you that?"

"She didn't have to. She has one just like it at home in England. Roses are my mother's favourite flowers."

"And her daughter's?"

"Not really. It's just that despite my newly discovered French blood, I can't bear to see things falling apart and neglected for the want of a little time and trouble."

"Ouch!"

"Well, it's true," Stephanie maintained. "Half the buildings here seem to be falling down."

"They've been doing that ever since I can remember. None of them, however, have actually done so."

"In Rouen—"

"They're renovating a whole lot of houses in Rouen. Didn't you notice? What about the rue du Gros Horloge? It's gleaming with new paint, or didn't you notice?"

"What about the Art School in the old charnel house?"

He shrugged. "Someone'll get around to it sooner or later. Perhaps they're waiting for you to put them right about it."

Stephanie snorted with rage. "Think what you like," she said at last, "it's your heritage that's falling apart with neglect, not mine!"

That seemed to amuse him. "You sound smug enough to be pure English," he teased her. "What a pity you're not!"

She beat about the bushes in increasing desperation. Arguing with him was not the best way to get rid of him, but she couldn't help it. It made her blood run faster and her heart pound against her ribs, but she still couldn't help it.

"I feel English!" She pushed her hair back with a grubby hand. "I don't want to be anything else! Though I can't see why it should matter to you, one way or the other!"

He advanced towards her and it was as much as she could do not to put a line of rose bushes between them as fast as possible.

"If you were only a *petite anglaise* and nothing more, I'd know where I was with you," he said.

"And where would that be?" she scoffed.

"I think it might be in your arms."

It was a second or two before she took in what he

had said. Her eyes widened with shock and she refused to meet his mocking gaze, feeling the hot colour in her cheeks.

"Frenchmen aren't nearly as romantic as they think they are," she retorted smoothly. "Nobody who fancies themselves as much as they do could be attractive to anyone else."

Pierre put out a hand and stopped her from stumbling over a concealed rose bush, considerably the worse for wear.

"You mustn't judge us all by Jean-Louis," he rebuked her. A smile curved his lips, fascinating her eye despite herself. "But then you don't, do you? Last night, it didn't matter to you at all that I was French—"

"I prefer to forget about last night!"

"Because your English dignity got ruffled?"

She sighed elaborately. "If you like. Anything you like. Last night was last night, and today is today. In between came the night, during which I was able to decide I don't need to have anything more to do with you. I don't need the hassle. I'm not even sure what I'm doing here."

"Staking your claim?"

"To what? A wilderness of roses planted by my mother? That's a question of sentiment. Besides," she added in a burst of honesty, "I'm hoping the Anders will have finished their breakfast and have gone to wherever it is that they came from before I get through with this!"

"Le Mans," he supplied.

"Le Mans what?"

"It's where they live," he explained patiently.

"I thought they raced cars there?"

"They do—for twenty-four hours, once a year. It's a place as well."

"I should think they absolutely hate it!" Stephanie murmured with enjoyment.

"They leave home for the duration."

"They would!"

"It's their one extravagance every year."

They both burst out laughing, and were as suddenly completely solemn again. Stephanie was reminded of how it had felt last night when he had swept her up into his arms and had kissed her breathless. It had been exciting, like a fireworks display in her head, and she had longed for it to go on forever. But it wouldn't do to let such thoughts dwell inside her. What if they were to take over altogether, as she feared they might? She stared at him, appalled, unable to move as he took a step closer to her, pushing her hair back out of her eyes with a careless, intimate hand.

"What makes you think this was your mother's garden?" he asked her.

She licked dry lips. "The roses are all her old favourites. While I'm here, I'll untangle some of the weeds. It'll give me something to do."

"I think we can find enough for you to do without that," he commented. "The Anders will be gone by lunchtime, and if you ask me, most of those roses have reverted to the wild and are beyond your help."

She glanced about her, because anything was better than looking at him, and saw the truth in what he was saying. Years of neglect had brought about a tangle more worthy of guarding a Sleeping Beauty than being turned back into a neat, English rose garden.

"Oh well," she sighed, "I could start again, I suppose." Her glance flickered to his face and away again, but not before she had caught the sympathy in the back of his eyes. It was as if he knew the ache of homesickness she had felt at the sight of the garden and, despite his lack of interest in it, had shared her longing to at least restore order in this small corner of her new country. "We like our gardens orderly and well-cared for in England," she said.

"I'm afraid Tante Janine is no gardener of any kind! One day I'll show you mine, and you can see what you think of that."

That caught equally at her interest and her heart-strings. "I didn't realise you had a garden," she said.

"I was too busy showing you the house last night."

The colour rose in her cheeks and she turned away from him. "I'd like to see the garden sometime," she murmured, confused.

"And what about the rest of it?"

She ignored that. "It will have to be soon. There's nothing to keep me here now that the Anders have been defeated, is there? I'll be going back to Rouen and settling in to my classes. Of course, I'll try to get over to see Grandmère from time to time, but it's a long way to come—"

"I doubt she'll let you go."

Stephanie hadn't thought of that. "She can hardly keep me here against my will!"

His smile was wry. "You play the part of the disinterested new relation very well. I could almost believe that you hadn't thought of all the possibilities long ago, except for one thing."

"What possibilities?" she demanded.

He looked at her sceptically. "Haven't you understood that the manor comes to you?"

She blanched. "Why me?"

"You're your father's daughter."

She swallowed, feeling as if her whole world had come unstuck in her hands. "I realised my being here put a spoke in my delightful relatives' wheel, but the house can't possibly be mine! I only learnt I had a French father and grandmother a few weeks ago. Inside, I'm still me, Stephanie Ironside! My stepfather left me very adequately provided for—and he's always been my father, not some stranger who died before I was even born!"

Pierre made an impatient movement. "Your eyes lit up when you saw the manor," he accused.

"Well of course, it's beautiful! A lovely place to visit, but I wouldn't want to live here! Grandmère is more than welcome!" She shook her head with decision. "I like going abroad for holidays, but not to *live!*" she added firmly. "Different customs are fun for a while, intriguing even, but for every day give me the familiar every time! Who would there be to laugh with here?"

Pierre's lips twitched. "We do laugh—quite a bit."

"Not with the Anders about!" she denied stoutly.

He looked amused. "You'll have to stay around until they've verified your claim, or Tante Janine'll be back where she started. Greedy people will go to any lengths to get their hands on what they feel is rightfully theirs. They'll have you investigated within an inch of your life, but you're not going to desert us now, are you?"

Stephanie picked at her torn finger. "I don't

know," she said at last. "I'm not sure I have the right to walk into somebody else's family quarrel. One can't like that dreadful family, but for all I know they may be right. Perhaps Grandmère would be better off in Paris. If the house is damp now in high summer, whatever is it like in the middle of winter?"

"Why don't you stay and find out?"

"Why should I? It's nothing to do with me!"

He raised his brows. "Your own grandmother?"

"Oh, you know what I mean!" she exclaimed. "I suppose I don't want to get involved. It doesn't seem to be anything to do with me."

"There could be another reason for staying." His voice lowered into a growl that rasped her nerves, setting them quivering with a new awareness that was not at all unpleasant, if unexpected.

"My life is settled—"

His laughter was more unnerving still. "How old are you, for heaven's sake?" he demanded.

"I don't see that as any of your business!"

"I'm making it mine. How old, Stephanie?"

"Twenty-two," she reluctantly revealed.

He grunted with satisfaction. "Young enough to adapt—"

"I don't want to adapt! If you want to know, I don't much like the French!"

"Then why did you contemplate marrying one?"

Why had she? It had been obvious at the time. She had thought she was in love with Jean-Louis, though why she should have thought anything so stupid was hardly a reason for self-congratulation when she thought about it now.

"An aberration—"

"Dear heart, it must have been more than that!"

She thought about it. "I don't think it was. Something must have made me think he was someone special—"

"Was he the first man you ever fell for?" Pierre suggested, amused by her honesty.

"No, of course not." Her laughter reached her eyes. "My mother fears that I'm incorrigibly susceptible, I run through dates at such a rate. *That* was the one thing in Jean-Louis' favour as far as she was concerned. He lasted so much longer than any of the others!"

"Only to lose you in the end?"

She shrugged. "That was his choice. He thought me too unsophisticated to be a diplomat's wife. What he meant," she added with a twisted smile, "was that I didn't know my place. When you French are formal, you outdo we British anytime!"

Pierre stood back and looked her over, starting at the crown of her head and ending with her neatly shod feet. Stephanie stirred restively under his gaze, more embarrassed than she wanted to admit, even to herself.

"If you ask me the man's a fool!" Pierre decided.

She dropped him a curtsy. "Thank you, kind sir, but I think he was right. He was constantly embarrassed in my company. I called his superior by his Christian name and he nearly collapsed in a heap on the floor!"

Pierre folded his arms across his chest. "I suppose you knew him well?"

"All my life."

A smile glimmered in Pierre's dark eyes. "Did he know that?"

Stephanie put an innocent expression on her face. "Should I have told him, do you think?"

"I think you're better off without him!"

It had taken a long time to reach that conclusion herself, but Stephanie found that no matter how hard she poked at the wound Jean-Louis had dealt her, there was no pain left, nothing but a sadness that she'd wasted so much time and heartbreak over someone who she didn't much like, if the truth were told.

"How do you know?" she said aloud. "He was considered to be the catch of the season—"

"Not for you!"

She raised her brows in mute enquiry. "He spoke English with the most charming accent imaginable!"

Pierre advanced on her so suddenly that she had no time to elude his embrace. He linked his fingers together behind her back, holding her easily as he smiled down at her.

"You speak French with a charming accent also, but I wouldn't kiss you for that!"

"I hope you're not going to kiss me at all!" she dared him.

"A forlorn hope, *petite*. I find you irresistible with the sun on your hair and that challenge in your eyes!"

"Then you'd better get it over with quickly! I have better things to do with my time than dally with you in the rose garden!"

"Have you?"

The sparkle left her face as his arms tightened

about her. What had been a joke was a joke no longer. Her breath was painfully suspended in her throat as she glimpsed the naked male aggression in his eyes. He had intended this all along! Well, that was hardly a surprise, and yet she felt paralysed by a new fear, a fear that she belatedly recognised to be her own reactions to this particular man. Dallying in the rose garden was the name she had given to what she had thought was a game, but now she knew it wasn't that at all. This was one of the most serious moments of her life and she couldn't bear for it to mean so little to him that he could toss it aside afterwards and never think of it again.

"I'm going in to breakfast!" she declared.

"Running away?"

She paused, poised for flight. "Yes," she admitted. "I don't want to get involved!"

His expression was kind. "You are involved, *petite*. There's nothing you can do about it now."

"I don't have to have anything to do with you!"

"Don't you?"

There was a touch of mockery in his voice that did nothing to allay the panic inside her. She opened her eyes wide. There had to be a way to put him in his place once and for all! She had to cut off the dangerous flow of electricity between them!

But he gave her no time to think of it. The pressure of his hands brought her tight up against him and, whilst she might have escaped his kiss if she had had her wits about her, she was paralysed by her own response to his hard male body. She shuddered with the excitement his touch engendered, shaking her head.

"All or nothing, *chèrie*," he murmured against her lips. She closed them firmly against him, annoyed by the thread of laughter she detected in his voice. She wasn't the spineless puppet he thought she was!

His teeth closed on her lower lip, giving it a small shake, and she was defeated. Her mouth opened to his, all thought of further defiance forgotten. She pressed closer against him, relishing the feel of his hard muscles beneath her fingers. If she wasn't careful she would lose her head completely, as she very nearly had last night. Why couldn't she get the message that this man was dangerous? She should have known better, she thought with self-contempt. Any man—only Pierre wasn't *any* man! The horrible conviction was growing inside her that Pierre was someone very special as far as she was concerned, that after him no other man would do. For an instant she was scared stiff, and then his kiss filled up her senses to the exclusion of all else. She couldn't get enough of him—but what did she mean to him?

When he released her she had a job to stand up straight on her own. She shivered and hugged herself to give herself confidence against the look of male triumph she detected in his eyes.

"It was only a kiss!" she muttered more to herself than to him.

"Only?"

"Can you honestly claim it was anything more?"

She would have taken back the challenge as soon as she'd uttered it, but it was already too late.

"Try this for size!" he said, taking her back in his arms.

His embrace was like a branding iron, writing his

name on her lips. She tried to shrug it off, but she knew she couldn't. Never again would she be plain Stephanie Ironside, enjoying a light flirtation as much as any other girl; from now on she would feel this man's claim on her whether he was there or not. It was the last thing she wanted, but she no longer had a choice in the matter. If Pierre wanted to take this further, she very much doubted that she would be able to prevent him. Her willpower had vanished in the excitement of being held with a firmness that in any other man she knew she would have resented. This was completion, a finding of herself in him that she had known nothing about before!

She took a deep breath, making a conscious effort to hide her unexpected discovery from Pierre's eyes as they scanned her flushed face. They were so wrapped up in each other that an outraged sound from the other side of the roses caught them both by surprise.

"I knew it!" Berthe exclaimed. "I knew she could never be the lost granddaughter! It was too convenient for her to be produced like a rabbit out of a hat just now! You might deceive Tante Janine with your floozie, Pierre, but you can't deceive me!"

"I wouldn't try," Pierre replied.

Stephanie's eyes opened wide at the note in his voice. If she were Berthe she would have backed down then and there, but Berthe had the courage of the stupid and saw no danger in pressing home her advantage.

"I'll call the others!" she threatened.

"Go right ahead," Pierre invited her. "But don't expect them to thank you."

Berthe sniffed. "Your girlfriend doesn't have much

to say for herself, does she? How much did you pay her to get the house for yourself, Pierre?"

Stephanie lost her temper with a suddenness that caught her as much by surprise as it did the other two.

"What did you want me to say?" she asked sweetly. "That I'd stand by and watch you and your family take my grandmother's home away from her? You'll have quite a lot of explaining to do when my identity is established. Meanwhile, would you mind removing yourself from my mother's rose garden? If I have to be French, at least I'm going to restore the little bit of England she brought here, and you have your foot on one of my favourites—perhaps you hadn't noticed?"

Berthe angrily removed her foot out of the flower-bed. "It's so over-grown it's impossible to see the paths!" she complained. "The rest of the house is no better! *We* only had Tante Janine's interests at heart. What will you do for her?"

Stephanie put her head on one side, considering the other woman with increasing distaste.

"I've always wanted a grandmother to love," she said.

Berthe choked over her contempt for such an emotion. "There's no money! Only what's tied up in that house! Ask anyone if you don't believe me!"

"To Grandmère it's her home!"

Berthe turned an unbecoming shade of brick red. "It isn't her home any longer, you silly girl! If you're who you say you are, the house is yours! You'll soon get tired of dancing round the old lady when you have to live with her. You'll see the wisdom then of putting her in a home where she can't do any more harm to anyone—"

"What harm has she ever done?" Stephanie demanded.

Berthe's eyes darkened with malice. "If she hadn't insisted on going on living here, we would have had our share ages ago. It isn't right that one person should have so much, especially as she doesn't use any of it to advantage. What does she need with all that expensive furniture at her age?"

Stephanie froze, remembering the labels the Anders had been affixing to the various pieces of furniture the evening before.

"I don't want anything from Grandmère, and nobody else is going to take her home away from her if I can help it." She looked Berthe squarely in the eyes. "You'd better tell your family they've had a wasted journey. Over my dead body will any of you get anything!"

"That's the spirit!" Pierre cheered her on.

She had forgotten for the moment that he was there. She turned on him. "You're not going to get it either!" she snapped at him.

He spread his hands in a very Gallic gesture. "*Petite*, what would I want with your grandmother's house?"

Stephanie frowned back at him. She supposed the old manor house was valuable or the Anders wouldn't be there, but she had to admit that Pierre's house was very much more to her taste. It would be nice to believe that he was genuinely concerned for the old lady who had taken him in and given him a home, and not on the make like the others, but she had to remember that she didn't know anything about him, not really.

His eyes filled with amusement. "You know one thing about me," he reminded her, as if she had spoken the thought aloud.

She sent him a look of enquiry before turning her attention back to Berthe.

"Where is the rest of your charming family?" she asked her.

Berthe sniffed and turned on her heel, hurrying away back to the house, bursting to tell the others what she had discovered in the rose garden.

"You've made an enemy there," Pierre observed.

Stephanie nodded. "I wouldn't want her as a friend, so it could be worse."

"What about me?" he said.

"What about you?"

"Don't you want me as a friend? Or do you fancy me enough to have me as a lover?"

Stephanie swayed where she stood. "I'll let you know," she said aloud, "if I make up my mind about you before I go back to England."

He put out a hand and patted her gently on the cheek. "Better hurry up, my love," he warned her, "or I may be tempted to make up your mind for you."

Chapter Six

Stephanie had always believed that a Frenchman's requirements for breakfast were comparatively modest, something like coffee and a roll smothered in jam. This was not true of the Anders family. They sat round the table, contemplating the pile of croissants in front of them with anticipation. They didn't, François was eager to explain, go to such extravagance when they were at home. He didn't believe in paying more than was necessary on the health and welfare of his family. His sister-in-law managed to contain her impatience quite successfully until he reached for his third croissant. Just then Berthe came running in from the garden, bursting with the news that whoever Stephanie was, there was something going on between her and Pierre. The Anders roared in unison with ill-concealed delight as Berthe dropped her bombshell.

"You'll have to listen to us now!" François exclaimed. "Pierre is obviously pulling a fast one, my dear. Is it likely that his girlfriend will turn out to be your granddaughter? He wants the house for himself, that's what it is!"

"Pierre only met the girl yesterday," Janine demurred.

"It didn't look like that to me!" Berthe said with a smugness that sat ill on her plain face.

Janine sighed. "Even if they've been keeping company for years that doesn't make her less my granddaughter, does it?"

"If you'll believe that, you'll believe anything!" Berthe chided her. "My dear, you'll have to face facts sooner or later. Pierre has always wanted to come between you and your real family. He's found this girl, heaven knows where, and he hopes to pass her off as your long-lost granddaughter. You did a bad thing when you took that young man into your household. We told you so at the time, but you wouldn't believe us. Let's hope you believe us now, before it's too late and you lose this wonderful opportunity to make your home in Paris where you'll be well looked after and won't have a thing to worry about in your old age."

Janine made a moue of distaste. "Won't I? How dull!"

"You shouldn't have to worry about this old house at your age," Berthe pressed her point. "We're none of us getting any younger."

Stephanie was just in time to hear this last re-
mark. She slipped into her place at the table with
a word of apology to her grandmother. Looking
round at the others, she could see that Berthe
hadn't been slow to report the incident she had
witnessed in the rose garden. Stephanie straightened her shoulders and looked down her nose at
the Anders, no longer caring if they knew she despised them for the mean tightwads she knew them
to be.

"I'm going to reclaim my mother's garden if you
don't mind," she announced to her grandmother.
"It's sadly neglected, but some of the bushes will
recover. It's the most English thing I've seen since I
got here."

"Your mother's garden?" François demurred.

"It was obviously designed and planted by her,"
Stephanie squashed him. "It's almost identical to the
one she has at home. All her favourite roses are out
there, struggling with the weeds. It's obvious you're
no gardener, Grandmère."

Her grandmother grinned delightedly. "You've
caught me out there, *ma petite*. I meant to keep the
garden exactly as your mother had it, as your father
would have wished." She sighed. "He was very proud
of the English rose garden, not that he would've kept
it any better than I have. Do as you like, *chérie,* this is
as much your home as mine!"

Stephanie blinked. "I don't want to take your home
away from you!" she protested. "I'll be going back to
England—"

"You took the trouble to learn French remarkably
well for an English girl who has no wish to live in

France!" Berthe observed, her small, black eyes narrowing with dislike.

"I was engaged to a Frenchman," Stephanie found herself saying. She hadn't meant to make any such admission.

"I suppose that was when Pierre met you?"

Astonished, Stephanie turned her head towards her. She had seldom been the victim of anyone's dislike before and she found the sensation uncomfortable and unsettling.

"No, I didn't know Pierre in those days," she said.

"Are you sure the truth isn't that Pierre looked the better bet—especially when he put you up to playing at being Tante Janine's granddaughter? It would be quite something if you could get this house *and* Pierre, wouldn't it?"

"The house is damp," Stephanie answered.

"I thought the English all lived in damp houses. You must be used to it by now."

"My home in England is perfectly dry."

"Then why are you so set on marrying a Frenchman?"

Stephanie began to laugh. "Believe me, once bitten, twice shy. The last thing I want to do is marry a foreigner after Jean-Louis—"

"He was the man you were going to marry?"

Stephanie nodded. "Jean-Louis Lourain, diplomat." Her eyes danced. "And stuffed shirt," she added, warming to her theme. "He convinced me once and for all that I don't want to marry a foreigner. I don't want to speak a foreign language all my life, and least of all do I want to be a mother to a brood of foreign children who can't speak my language properly and can't understand my jokes. That's what I learned from Jean-Louis, and I learned the lesson well. Besides everything else, he's a snob. When I marry, I'll take care it isn't to anyone who considers himself above my station in life. I was worn-out being grateful for Jean-Louis' notice by the time he'd decided I didn't know my place well enough to be a diplomat's wife. All I could feel was relief that I didn't have to go through with it. Oh no, no Frenchmen for me!"

Only her grandmother laughed. "He sounds perfectly horrid," she agreed, "though he did teach you to speak excellent French—"

"Never at a loss for a word, is she?" Pierre agreed, coming languidly into the room. "Are those croissants going begging, or is someone else going to eat them?"

Stephanie decided it was time for her to assert herself. "One of them's mine!" she insisted.

Pierre tested them for warmth against his knuckles, picked out the largest and fluffiest of those that were left and placed it on the plate in front of her.

"You have to look after yourself when the Anders are about," he advised her. "Help yourself to coffee and give me some too, will you?"

He sat down beside her, hooking one foot over the bar of her chair in an action that was more intimate than she liked. She could feel her cheeks growing hot, and resented the impression they must be giving to her reluctant relatives.

"Are you always here for breakfast?" she asked him.

He grinned at her. "It depends on what attractions

are on offer over here. Tante Janine usually begins the
day in her room and isn't on show before lunchtime."

"We don't flatter ourselves that we're the attraction
today," Berthe smirked across the table.

"No," Pierre agreed. His eyes met Berthe's in a
head-on clash. "We've never had anything to say to
one another, though at one time I think you thought
we had."

Berthe backed down, casting an uncomfortable
sideways glance at her husband to see if he were
listening. "It wasn't entirely my imagination," she
declared angrily. "You always wanted jam as well as
butter on your bread, and in those days you weren't
even sure of the bread!"

"My family didn't leave me penniless," Pierre
pointed out in kindly tones.

"We weren't to know that! Tante Janine paid for
everything you needed as a child—"

Annoyed, Tante Janine's mouth tightened into a
disapproving line. "Pierre is my second son. Please
remember that, all of you!"

François stabbed the air with the remains of his
croissant, looking unbelievably pompous.

"Now, now, dear lady, we only have your best
interests at heart. This young man has always sponged
on you and he isn't really family at all. Oh, I know
he's a distant connection of *yours,* but he's nothing to
do with *us* at all. You can't object to our putting real
family first. I think Berthe may be right that Pierre is
trying to foist this young lady onto you for some
nefarious reason of his own. I shall make enquiries at
once as to who she really is." He looked round the

table complacently. "As the head of the family, it's my place to see that nobody takes advantage of you. It'd be madness for you to pass up this opportunity of making your home in Paris, and I can't condone anyone trying to persuade you otherwise. We could all do with the money that the sale of this place would bring. Stephanie—it is Stephanie, isn't it?—will surely understand that we find her claim unbelievable at first sight, especially as she gets along so very well with Pierre, whom none of us have ever seen any reason to trust or respect. It's only right she should have to prove her identity beyond doubt. Every court in the land will uphold me in that!"

Stephanie longed for Pierre to demolish the man, but he went on lounging in his chair, a faint smile on his lips, saying nothing at all. She cast him an indignant look, but he only shrugged his shoulders, nodding towards her grandmother as if warning her to be careful.

Stephanie sat up very straight and prepared to do battle on her own behalf. "I won't have you upsetting my mother," she warned the older man. "Make all the enquiries you want to, but if I hear from her that you've been trying to bully her as you have my grandmother, this'll be the last time you ever set foot inside this house. Is that clear?"

"Your mother's probably in this too—" François growled angrily.

"My mother is recently widowed and has enough problems of her own. I'll give you the name of our lawyer and you can make your enquiries of him. I mean what I say, monsieur *mon oncle,* so be careful how you proceed."

Pierre silently clapped his hands. "Bravo! It takes an Anders to deal with one!"

Stephanie turned on him. "And what's that supposed to mean?"

"I thought you didn't want any part of this house?"

"I don't!"

"It sounded like it," he murmured.

Stephanie's eyes filled with angry tears. "Would you rather they had it?"

Janine's face pinched with disappointed anger. "Children, children, if you must fight each other, go and do it somewhere else. It makes me tired to listen to you. For the moment no one can do anything and let's leave it like that. I have my home and you have your enquiries to make. Stephanie will not object to spending a short holiday with her grandmother, I'm sure, whatever the outcome, and Pierre can help me entertain her—without quarreling, *mon fils*, or I'll have something to say about the matter. Stephanie is not to blame for things that happened in the past and which she knows nothing about. Is that clear?"

"Admirably so, Tante," Pierre agreed with a wry smile. He stretched his arms lazily above his head, giving Stephanie a fine view of a darkly tanned midriff that made her senses jump. "Stephanie has nothing to fear from me—"

"As long as everything goes your way!" Stephanie shot at him.

"Quite right," he murmured, transferring his smile to her. "As long as Tante Janine is left in peace, we'll get along very well. We do already, don't we?"

"Do we?" Stephanie was pleased with her casual answer, more pleased yet that she could raise an amused eyebrow as she stared him down. She wasn't the easy meat he thought she was.

Stephanie went back to the rose garden straight after breakfast. She wondered if she should have hung around to say goodbye to the Anders, but she hardly felt they would miss her—any of them. It seemed odd to think that she had anything to do with this remote part of France, let alone that her father had been born and raised there. But if he had had to die, he should have gone completely, and not reached out to her after all these years, drawing her into a complicated knot of relationships she was sure she would be far better off without. Would her mother be distressed by this unlikely turn of events? It was hard sometimes to know what her mother was feeling and thinking, harder still to imagine her in her younger days as the distraught widow of a Frenchman. Stephanie couldn't remember her as anything other than the socially competent, rather cool Mrs. Ironside who had never really been close to anyone at all.

The roses were in a worse state than she had thought. She was a fool for trying to make any impression on them. As soon as she was gone they would be as neglected as ever, and no one would be able to tell that she had passed that way. Perhaps it was all a figment of her imagination.

The earth smelled sweet, however, and the scent of the roses was soothing as she wrestled with their brambles. It was better to be doing something rather than nothing, though she was not naturally a gardener. How her mother would have laughed to have seen her now!

By the time she had reduced a single bed to order she was hot and tired, and more than ready to call it a day. The thorns had lacerated her hands and it took her a little while to remove their tips from her reddened skin. What she needed was a shower and a change of clothing. After that, she would have a long talk with her grandmother. She just hoped the other woman wouldn't think it cheek on her part to want to get something settled between them. Rouen beckoned, and she didn't want to lose the opportunity of a lifetime because she hadn't the courage to tell her new family that she wanted no part of her real father's heritage. She had enough to handle being Stephanie Ironside and coping with her mother's objections to her tackling anything as insecure as a career in design.

Stephanie's lips twisted in dismay, remembering when she had discovered that what her mother had really wanted was for her to stay at home and be a companion to her. There was plenty for her to do, her mother had insisted, carving out a social life for herself and finding herself a suitable husband. Stephanie had wondered at the time why her mother had thought it so important that she should marry wealth and success. Now she thought she knew. Her mother might have been madly in love with her Frenchman, but he hadn't made her happy. Had she felt a stranger in a foreign land before her husband had gone away to war and got himself killed? Was this rose garden a silent memorial to the hours of loneliness and despair her mother had suffered whilst she had lived in the old manor house?

Picking out a last thorn, Stephanie walked round the moated house to the front door and into the hallway. She was astonished to find Pierre on his hands and knees, apparently staring into space.

"What are you doing?" she asked him.

He shushed her with a gesture. "I don't want Tante Janine to see these labels. Help me get them off, will you?"

Stephanie set to with a will, joining him on the floor.

"What kind of people are they, these relatives I didn't know I had?" she muttered crossly.

"The Anders have always been greedy," he replied calmly.

"Are you?"

He grinned amiably at her. "I'm not an Anders—not by birth. I infinitely prefer Tante Janine's side of the family."

"I'm not surprised!"

He paused in what he was doing, catching hold of one of her thorn-torn hands and making her wince in the process.

"Are *you* greedy, Stephanie?" His fingers caressed the palm of her hand as he watched her carefully, his expression unreadable. "Are you going to turn Tante Janine out of her home and take possession of it for yourself?"

"Good gracious, no!"

"Then what are you going to do about her?"

"I don't see why I should do anything. I didn't even know she existed until yesterday. I don't mind putting a spoke in the wheel of her family by making sure they can't turn her out, but I don't want to have anything more to do with it myself. I have my own life to lead!"

"Oh yes? Tell me about that life."

"There isn't much to tell—"

"Tell me about Jean-Louis!"

She struggled to regain possession of her hand, but he held it too tightly for her to win free unless she insisted, and she didn't feel strong enough for that. She liked being in contact with him. She would have liked to have been closer still. And that all added up to danger, she told herself, but she still didn't do anything about it.

"Jean-Louis's a Frenchman. Enough said." She managed a light laugh and jumped to her feet, pulling him up after her.

"You have something against Frenchmen?" he asked innocently.

"Too right I have!"

His expression was innocent. "Something against *me?*"

"You're a Frenchman, aren't you?"

"I'm not Jean-Louis. Tell me about him, Stephanie."

"There's nothing to tell. I made a mistake. I took him at face value, romantic image, the Gallic charm, the lot! It was hardly his fault that he turned out to be a humourless poke! He did me a favour in a way. I'll never believe all those stories about how romantic the French are ever again!"

"Never?"

She shook her head violently. "I'm immune!" she claimed. "I'll never be taken in again! The sooner I get back to Englishmen the better!"

He laughed softly in the back of his throat. "Then what are you doing here, *petite?*"

"I was kidnapped by you, remember?"

"Can't you learn to paint in England?"

She was taken off balance. "It was an opportunity to widen my horizons," she began. She laughed also with a self-mockery that hurt. "I'd spent so much time perfecting my French, I was hanged if I was going to let it all go to waste. It hasn't been much fun at home since Daddy died."

"Your stepfather?"

She pulled away from him. "He was the only father I knew! Is it surprising I miss him?"

Pierre's eyes never left her face. "Do you know, I don't believe you miss him all that much. You don't give the impression that you're used to having much emotion in your everyday life at all. Perhaps that's why you set your cap at Jean-Louis? He wouldn't demand too much of you, would he?"

Stephanie shuddered. "My family in England is more civilised than this one! That doesn't mean we feel less!"

"Prove it!" he challenged her.

She turned away, more shaken than she wanted to admit. How could one prove such a thing?

"I'm going to find my grandmother," she announced. "She might have something sensible to say about what she plans to do now." She turned back to Pierre, her eyes wide. "Have you any objection?"

"Why should I?" he retorted.

"I don't know." She decided to be truthful. "I get the impression that you don't trust me around her. I won't do her any harm you know. I don't want her house or furniture. I don't want anything from her."

"Don't you?"

Stephanie spread her hands. "All right, what could I possibly want that I haven't already got?"

"An escape from your present life?" he suggested. His head was on one side as he looked at her, a smile pulling at the corner of his lips.

"I like my life as it is!" she declared.

"If you go back to England now it'll be as dull as it's always been," he mocked her. "What makes you think a nice, safe Englishman is what you want? You'd do better to stick around here and find out what life's all about."

"At your hands?" she concluded nastily. "Thanks, but no thanks."

"Don't dismiss it so lightly," he warned her. "You may not know it, Stephanie darling, but you're as ripe for a romantic adventure now as you'll ever be. What's more, your mother might want to keep you chained to the cool, passionless past, but your grandmother won't—"

"My mother has nothing to do with anything!"

"Hasn't she? I've always understood that she was afraid of her own shadow when it came to loving, completely out of her depth. Maybe her daughter's more like her than I thought?"

"And maybe you should brush up on that line of yours," she snapped back at him. "It's pure ham! You didn't know my mother, and you don't know me! I'm not passionless and I'm not greedy and—and it's none of your business what I am!"

He took a step towards her and she was very conscious of the threat he presented by his sheer masculinity. Half of her wanted to turn and run, but the other half relished the glow he brought to her skin, and the flutter in her heartbeat that refused to be brought back under her control. It was exciting to meet Pierre's challenge, more exciting than was good for her.

His hands came down on her shoulders, slipping down her back to her hips. "If you don't want the house, what do you want? Me?"

She opened her mouth to deny it and, too late, saw the trap she had fallen into. His lips took hers in a masterful assault, his tongue taking advantage of her outrage to seek and find hers, filling her mouth with the taste of him. She was hurtled from her momentary complacency to being out of control, a tool in his hands, eagerly compounding her own defeat. She sought to get closer still to him, to rub her fingers through the hair on his chest, unable to get enough of him as he deepened the kiss still further. He was holding her so close against him that she couldn't tell if it were his heartbeat or hers that was hammering against her ribs.

When he finally released her she gazed at him in wide-eyed wonder. His shirt was unbuttoned to the waist, revealing the dark tan she had caught a glimpse of at breakfast. Her eyes rose slowly to meet his. It was as if a charge of electricity was passing through her as she took in the male triumph his eyes revealed, and felt an answering weakness inside herself that settled disastrously in her knees as she battled to regain control over herself.

"You see how easy it would be?" Pierre mocked her gently.

She flicked her fingers, surprising herself when she

managed to make quite a sound with them. "A mere kiss!" she scoffed. "The French are good at that, but when it comes to perseverance, to sheer staying power, I'll take the English anytime!"

His eyes hardened. "Perhaps you want too much after all," he said.

"A Frenchman would think so!"

For a long moment they glared at each other, neither of them able to withdraw the challenge they offered to each other merely by being male and female. Pierre recovered first. He put a hand up to the back of his neck and rubbed hard under the collar of his shirt.

"You'd better go and find Tante Janine," he said at last. "I'll finish taking off these labels. If you want me, I'll be at home."

Stephanie nodded, still unable to wrench her gaze away from his. The sooner she found her grandmother and explained the urgency of her getting back to Rouen the better. Yet it took an effort of will to turn and walk away from this Frenchman. Later, it was to occur to her that it had cost her more to walk away from Pierre's embrace than it had to walk away from the prospect of a whole lifetime with Jean-Louis. But for now she would focus on her grandmother. She washed her face and hands vigorously in cold water, and made up afterwards with inordinate care. She would forget all about it, and then no one would ever know that she wasn't quite as convinced that her English blood was going to come out on top as she had been first thing that morning.

Chapter Seven

Stephanie's grandmother preferred a certain formality in her household of which Stephanie could only approve. It was quite different from the lack of real interest which had dominated her family life so far. She knew her grandmother to be more than fascinated by every detail of her childhood and how she thought and felt about everything, but there was no presumption that she had any right to pry into the younger woman's affairs, nor any word of criticism, or even advice unless she was specifically asked.

So it was that nearly a week slipped by without Stephanie being aware of the fact. She woke up on the fifth day of her visit in a state of panic.

"I must leave for Rouen today!" she told her grandmother over the breakfast table. "I can't miss this term at the Art School there. It would be ridiculous!"

"Not today, dear," her grandmother returned imperturbably. "We have a visitor today."

"We have?"

But the older woman had nothing further to say on the matter. She dismissed it as calmly as if Stephanie had taken leave of her senses and suggested they should visit the moon. As she ate her roll and jam and sipped at her coffee, Stephanie wondered how she could broach the subject again. If she didn't get to Rouen the next day she wouldn't be there in time to sign on for her course.

Only as she was rising from the table did her grandmother drop her final bombshell.

"I believe you're acquainted with Jean-Louis Louvain? I'd be obliged if you'd help to entertain him at luncheon today."

Stephanie stared. "Not on your life, Grandmère! I shall definitely make my way to Rouen this morning!"

"Running away?"

Stephanie regarded her, a mutinous twist to her lips. "You can call it anything you like, I will not see Jean-Louis again, not for anybody!"

Her grandmother's face softened with affection. "Were you so much in love with him, child?"

She hadn't loved him at all, Pierre had taught her that; but neither did she want to see him, to remind herself of all the dreams she had invested in a creature of her invention, for her version of Jean-Louis had born very little resemblance to the real man.

"I just don't want to see him," she said aloud.

"Your mother is anxious that you should."

"My mother?" *That* Stephanie could believe. Her mother had seized on Jean-Louis as an ideal son-in-law from the moment she had set eyes on him. She had been loud and long in her praise of him. He was sufficiently stable to be able to give her daughter a secure and happy life—and he was French. Her mother had always had a soft spot for the French that was ruthlessly suppressed in her husband's presence. Yet it was apt to surface at other, unexpected moments, such as the time she had dragged Stephanie halfway across London to see an exposition of the Norman way of life. Stephanie lifted her chin.

"Is he bringing his wife with him?" she asked.

"Apparently that was a mistake—"

Stephanie shook her head. "*I* was the mistake. It wouldn't have done his career any good to marry a foreigner, especially one who wouldn't stay in her proper place! He was remarkably clear on the subject."

Her grandmother sat down again. "But you're no longer a foreigner," she pointed out.

"I'll always be a foreigner!" Stephanie claimed extravagantly. "Blood doesn't mean much these days."

"It could mean your happiness—"

"With Jean-Louis?" Stephanie was stunned by the idea. She had come a long way since she had left the shores of her homeland, she thought. She put her head on one side and smiled. "You know, Grandmère, *my* Jean-Louis was the most beautiful man you've ever imagined. The real Jean-Louis may be rather a letdown for both of us."

"I see. Your mother thought you'd decided to escape to Rouen because you were unhappy. Wasn't that true?"

"In a way," Stephanie admitted. "It seemed to be one thing after another. First Jean-Louis, running out on me, and then Daddy dying. I wouldn't have come if I'd thought I could have been any help to Mama, but she seldom shows what she's feeling and I got the impression she didn't want me around."

"She was the same when Guy died," her grandmother remembered.

"Was she?" Stephanie wasn't much interested. She couldn't believe it had been quite the same. "She got very angry when I told her Daddy had said Jean-Louis was too charming for his own good, and that he was glad I wasn't marrying him. That was when she told me about my French father."

Janine looked thoughtful. "Perhaps she missed her life here more than I knew. At the time I thought only of my own loss—"

"Mama hasn't been unhappy. She lives a very social life and has masses of friends. She wouldn't have had that here, would she?"

"No," her grandmother agreed. "Here, if Guy had lived, she would have had love."

Stephanie had never considered the relationship between her parents before. "I think she received more love than she gave," she said at last. "She's always been cool and rather turned-in on herself. Daddy used to laugh at her and say she didn't believe in offering herself twice over as a hostage to fortune. Perhaps he knew about my real father?"

"It seems likely," her grandmother said dryly. "She

would've had to have had some explanation for your presence, hmm?"

Stephanie laughed reluctantly. "I suppose she would at that. She told me it was Daddy who didn't want me told about my real father. He wanted us to be a proper family. You'd have liked him. He worked far too hard to be at home much, especially when I was young. He'd shower us both with presents, whether we wanted them or not. He didn't like parties as Mama does, but he said they were the oil that made his business go smoothly."

Janine Anders looked more thoughtful still. "Tell me more about this Jean-Louis of yours," she commanded. "Does your mother like him?"

"He's French," Stephanie replied, as if that was all that needed to be said.

Her grandmother smiled a secret smile. "There are other Frenchmen in the world."

There was Pierre. The image of Pierre took possession of Stephanie's mind. He had stayed away from her and the house for the last few days, and she had begun to think she had succeeded in getting him into perspective. Again and again she had told herself that he was only a man and of no interest to her, and she had begun to believe it. Now, she was as conscious of his virile attraction as if he had been in the room alone with her.

"There are plenty of nice, safe Englishmen in the world too," she said aloud.

"You're too much like your mother to settle for safety," her grandmother remarked.

Stephanie gave her a startled look. "Mother worships safety!"

"Not the first time around."

It was a new thought for Stephanie. Had her
mother felt for her unknown father something akin to
what she had felt the first time she had seen Pierre? A
mixture of fright and pleasure that refused to go away
even now? She had never thought of her mother in
quite that light, but it all added up to her having been
badly hurt by Guy Anders' death. Perhaps she had
never recovered from the pain that had been dealt her
then. It certainly explained a lot about her second
marriage and her refusal to risk being hurt ever again.

"She still didn't have to send Jean-Louis here," she
groaned. "I told her that was all over."

"You couldn't have made a very convincing job of
it, *ma chère*. The young man himself seems to imagine
you'll be all over him when he gets here. Now why
should that be?"

Stephanie made a face. "You'll know when you see
him." She decided to go onto the attack. "You know,
Grandmère, I'm sure this is a plot to stop me going to
Rouen—"

Her grandmother was the picture of innocence.
"Whatever could have given you that idea?" she
asked.

Stephanie knew the instant Pierre came into the
room. She had cut some of her mother's roses for the
table and was arranging them in the only suitable bowl
she could find.

"Have you any idea of the value of that vase?"
Pierre asked her.

She turned to face him. "It'll be quite safe on the
table, won't it?"

His disapproval came in waves towards her. "Does Jean-Louis rate so much trouble on your part?"

"I didn't invite him," she reminded him.

"I understood it was for your benefit that he's coming," he grunted.

"So everyone seems to think," she nodded.

He looked at her sharply. "Put him off and come out with me instead," he suggested.

She shook her head. "I couldn't do that."

"No," he agreed, "I didn't think you would."

Quite suddenly the events of the day became too much for Stephanie and she lost her temper with a completeness that would have shocked her at any other time.

"I've never given any of you any reason to think you could order my life for me!" she let blaze at him. "Tomorrow, I'm going to Rouen and I'll be rid of the lot of you! Go away, and leave me alone!"

"Ah yes, Rouen," he drawled.

"What d'you mean by that?" she demanded.

"Tante Janine—"

Her green eyes were as fiery as emeralds in the sun. "I'll visit Grandmère from time to time. She can't ask more from me than that! I have my whole future life to consider!"

"In a French family, even today a well brought up young girl often has her whole life mapped out for her by her elders and betters," he warned her.

"Not me!"

His smile, to her eyes, was decidedly complacent. "Why not you?"

She eyed him demurely through her eyelashes.

"Because I don't think we could agree as to what a well brought up young girl is. I like me the way I am."

"And you think I don't?"

"I really don't care either way." It cost her quite an effort to remain cool and detatched from his probing. The effect he had on her was dismaying. She didn't only want to look at him, she wanted to touch him.

"You don't have to stay and see Jean-Louis," he reiterated. "Come with me instead!"

"To prove my independence?"

"For whatever reason you care to think up. I want you, Stephanie, and you want me. Why waste your time on this other fellow?"

"I was engaged to marry him!"

"So?"

"So I owe him a hearing, don't you think?"

"Not if you want me."

She was startled into looking fully at him. It was a mistake. He was unbearably familiar and dear to her. She knew exactly how his hair grew out of his scalp, and she would have recognised his hands anywhere, even if the rest of him was hidden from her. She didn't have to look at him to remember how it had felt to be in his arms. She was aware of it every moment of every day.

"What makes you think I want you?" she dared him.

It was her second mistake. He came towards her, taking her unresisting hands in hers. "This," he whispered softly against her lips and put his mouth against hers.

She tried so hard to resist the temptation of responding to the unspoken demand of his kiss. It occurred to her that she had never been tempted before to give back kiss for kiss and hang the consequences. Any embraces she had exchanged with Jean-Louis had been calm, formal incidents that had meant remarkably little to her. She had never felt the excitement of danger at the touch of any man. It was like a drug that could become a necessity to her if she didn't fight every inch of the way.

"I thought I was a grasping female, trying to deprive my grandmother of her house?" she murmured.

"Are you?" he retorted.

She frowned. "I don't want the house!"

"But you want me!" he triumphed. "What are you going to do about it?"

She released herself, drawing herself up to her full height, not that she need have bothered, for he was still a full head taller than she.

"I'm going to Rouen to get on with my own life," she told him sweetly. "It won't take long to forget all about you, I'm sure."

"Then I'll give you something to remember me by!"

He snatched her back against him and she was bitterly conscious of the warmth of his body and the message of need it relayed to her own clamouring senses. His kiss when it came was as soft as thistledown, to be overtaken a minute later by a passion that reduced her to a quivering response she couldn't begin to deny.

"Come home with me," he said again.

She smoothed down her clothes, wishing she could smooth out her emotions with the same ease. "If I do,

will you explain why to Grandmère?'' she mocked
him.

His eyes caught fire, cutting off her breath and
bringing a weakness to her knees. "I might, if you lack
the courage, *ma chère.*"

She almost told him that Jean-Louis was no more
than a ghost from the past. She wanted to badly. Then
she remembered that he hadn't taken her seriously
before, when she had told him that all Jean-Louis had
taught her was the French language and a vast distrust
for Frenchmen. Pierre didn't really take her seriously
at all. He thought he could charm her into doing
anything he wanted her to and that, more than
anything else, put some iron into her backbone.

"Perhaps I shall fall in love with Jean-Louis all over
again," she taunted him.

He looked at her long and soberly, and she wished
she knew what he was thinking. When he spoke, he
sounded quite different, as if he had made up his mind
about something and had decided that he could afford
to play a waiting game. It unnerved her; she felt that
somehow she would be the loser.

"Jean-Louis has had his chance. Don't flatter yourself it's you he's coming to woo, *ma petite*. You're
somebody quite different from the person he knew
before." He shrugged his shoulders. "Diplomats deal
in backgrounds. Is your Jean-Louis any different?"

Stephanie refused to give him the pleasure of seeing
he'd hit home.

"Jean-Louis is a gentleman," she said distantly.

"And I'm not?" He laughed. It wasn't a pleasant
sound and she wished her earlier words unsaid.
"Don't answer that!" he commanded. "At least I'm a

man, and that's something I can wait to prove to you, little coward. See your Jean-Louis and dream your dreams, and see where that gets you! You know where to find me when you want me—the only difference is that this time you'll have to come looking for me!"

He turned on his heel and walked out of the house without a backward glance, leaving Stephanie feeling both guilty and misunderstood. Men! They were the most upsetting creatures in the world! Pierre had succeeded in ruining her day, and now she had to face Jean-Louis who she had once thought had ruined her whole life. At least, this time round, Jean-Louis had no power to hurt her. He was nothing more than a nuisance. She wished she could say the same about Pierre!

Jean-Louis was some two inches shorter than she remembered him. His dress was a parody of the City of London gentleman, complete with rolled black umbrella and a hat that he brushed carefully as he took it off and set it on the hall table. Stephanie remembered that hat, and the times she had longed to put her foot through it when she had thought he paid it more attention than he did her. It had to be worn just so, at exactly the correct angle, though she had never understood why, as the only result had been to leave a line across his forehead. And yet she had never once questioned why he, a Frenchman, had felt the need to dress in a style that all the world knew as English, and old-fashioned English at that.

She had a hard job not to laugh as she took him in to present him to her grandmother, and recognised the old lady's disbelief that this could have been the man her granddaughter had almost married.

"This is Jean-Louis, Grandmère. Jean-Louis, may I present my grandmother, Madame Anders?"

"Enchanté," whispered Jean-Louis, impressed.

Madame Anders made no such polite greeting. "Guy would have shown him the door," she whispered to Stephanie. "What is your mother thinking about?"

"Jean-Louis is a high-flyer," Stephanie answered, trying not to laugh. "The diplomatic service is lucky to have him. He's going to be the French Ambassador at the Court of St. James, or even in Washington before he's through."

"Really?"

"I take my career very seriously, madame," Jean-Louis confirmed.

"Which is why you want to marry my granddaughter?"

Stephanie waited with interest to see how Jean-Louis would respond to the blunt question. He could at least have looked embarrassed, she thought, as he put a possessive hand on hers.

"I've always wanted to marry Stephanie," he said with a solemn sincerity that made him sound quite convincing. "It was unfortunate that she happened to be a foreigner, but now I've her mother's word that all that has changed! There's nothing to prevent the match now, is there, Stephanie?"

"Only one little thing," she smiled back at him. "When I marry, I want to be swept off my feet by my future husband, not rated as second best to his career prospects."

Jean-Louis patted her hand in a quite odious way. "You haven't thought about it properly," he chided her. "Romance is all very well in its place, but you've always had the best of everything and I can only provide for your future if I do the job I know best. You always understood that before!"

"I was dazzled," Stephanie murmured.

Her grandmother's eyes snapped with amusement. "Dazzled, *ma chère?*"

Stephanie managed an innocent look. "I'd always heard how romantic the French are, with their Gallic charm and their understanding of women. My mother always said so. It was some time before I discovered the truth for myself."

"What truth?" Jean-Louis demanded, bewildered.

"Why, what you've just been saying, *mon chèr*, that the French don't really believe in romance at all. They have a proper sense of priorities, like marriage, and the importance of keeping a firm eye on the future. How many times have I heard you say that our children would have to be kept away from the hoi-polloi? Their marital chances were to be considered from the moment of birth—no, before that!—by bearing in mind the suitability of their mother for the task!"

"I see." Madame Anders was still amused. "The families of the ancien régime may guard their blood-lines, but the rest of us allow the heart a place in our alliances—"

"A very practical place, judging by your own family!" Stephanie exclaimed.

"Ah, but, *ma fille,* the heart doesn't always fall for another member of the human race. It can fall in love with gold, or possessions, or even an old and beautiful house—"

"Or a job!" Stephanie concluded for her.

The old lady nodded. "That too." She turned to Jean-Louis, extending him her hand and watching critically as he bowed impatiently over it. "You must forgive me, young man, but I understood from my granddaughter you were betrothed to someone else? Did I make a mistake, or did she—or did my daughter-in-law, in thinking you wanted to renew your engagement to Stephanie?"

Jean-Louis was happy and eager to explain. "Stephanie's the only girl I want to marry, madame, I can assure you of that. There were a few difficulties, brought about mostly by her father—er—stepfather, I'm bound to say for selfish reasons, in that he didn't want to be parted from Stephanie while she travelled with me all over the world. He tried to break us up from the very beginning, and he very nearly succeeded by pointing out to me what a disadvantage it would be for a diplomat to marry a foreign citizen. I had hopes, however, that Stephanie would take up French nationality, but she refused. She can hardly do so now. She is French, whatever she likes to think, and so there's no longer any problem on that score."

"At most I'm half-French!" Stephanie retorted. "I feel English, and that's what I want to be! Daddy was right. He said I found the business world bad enough, but I'd feel like a fish out of water in the diplomatic world. He said he'd always wanted the best for my mother, but she'd never told him what the best thing for her was, so he stayed doing what he knew best. He wanted me to marry an artist, or someone like that."

"Your mother doesn't agree with him," Jean-Louis said sulkily. "He's dead, and he's nothing to do with you really. That's why I came."

"My mother," Stephanie pointed out gently, "isn't me."

"You were in love with me before!"

"I was in love with love. You had very little to do with it."

Jean-Louis made an angry movement. "I suppose you feel you have to tease me a little. Well, I can take it, knowing what I do about you. Your French is really very good now, my dear. Congratulations."

Stephanie's smile was quizzical. "Thank you."

He dismissed her with a nod and she wondered if he had always been so pompous. It seemed incredible to her that she had ever had more than a warm affection for him. What could she have been thinking of to imagine that she'd been in love with him?

She hardly took part in the conversation after that. Her grandmother struggled alone, occasionally casting an angry look in her granddaughter's direction. Once, as they were going in to lunch, she muttered her annoyance, "The young man came to see you, Stephanie, not me!"

"Ah, but I didn't invite him," Stephanie retorted.

That made her grandmother crosser still. "I thought I was doing you a favour. Your mother seemed to think so!"

Stephanie's only answer was a wicked grin, but she did make some effort after that to entertain the luckless Jean-Louis, still marveling that he showed no sign that he knew his presence to be unwelcome to her.

After lunch, his one wish was to be shown over the house.

"You take him, Stephanie," her grandmother entreated her. "There are times these days when I feel remarkably old. It's your house, after all."

Stephanie kissed her lightly on the cheek. "No, Grandmère, it is yours for as long as you live."

Jean-Louis watched the scene with indulgence. "Very proper," he agreed. "You won't have any need of the house for many years yet."

Stephanie sighed. She would speak to him when they were alone, she decided, and began to look forward to showing him over the house with some relish. Looking back on their past relationship she remembered she had seldom been able to get a word in edgeways, but this time round she meant to hold the floor and put him firmly in his place, so that even he wouldn't be able to misunderstand her intentions ever again.

"We'll start in the dairy," she suggested. "You see, these houses are really old farmsteads, and not manor houses at all. They're working houses—even this one, despite the moat and the age of the beams. It looks quite like an English house of the same period, doesn't it?"

"It's French," he objected, creasing his brow.

"Norman," she corrected him. "Normandy has a lot in common with England."

"Normandy is France!"

She ushered him into the dairy, watching him as he looked about with appreciation. She could almost see the wheels going round in his brain as he put a value on everything he saw.

"Don't count your chickens before they're hatched," she advised him. "I seem to have found myself a whole new family and they'll all be looking for some way to break my father's will. They want Grandmère to live in a home in Paris."

"That might be the best thing for her—"

"I don't think so," she cut him off. "I think it'd kill her."

His mouth tightened. "You always did think you knew best about everything! It seems more likely her family would know what's best for her." He caught up with himself. "What d'you mean the house may not be yours? Your mother seemed quite certain."

"I have to prove that I'm my father's daughter. I'm not sure I want to," she explained.

"But Stephanie, then we'll be back to where we were before! I had to go to a lot of trouble to get time off to come here and put things right with you. I expected you to be pleased that we can marry—"

Stephanie turned to face him. "You haven't even kissed me, Jean-Louis," she pointed out. "What sort of marriage would it be?"

"You never much cared for that sort of thing," he muttered. "How am I supposed to catch up with your moods?"

"D'you want to kiss me?" she asked with curiosity.

"Well, of course I do! Come here and I'll show you."

She chewed thoughtfully on her lower lip. "Why don't you come to me?" she dared him.

His kiss was a sober affair that left her as unmoved as if he had shaken her by the hand.

"I don't think it's going to work out, do you?" she said, almost sadly.

"You're not trying!" he complained. "You never did much care for that side of things!"

So it was her fault! Her annoyance flared and died. She put her arms round his neck and kissed him softly on the lips. She knew she was kissing him goodbye, and she hoped he knew it too.

"It was kind of you to come," she said, "but I'm sure the other girl will make you a much better wife."

Jean-Louis turned brick red. "There isn't any other girl," he confessed.

Stephanie didn't know what she would have done then. She had no time to find out. She was wrenched out of Jean-Louis' embrace and shoved out of the dairy door with such little ceremony that she didn't even have the time to object or to fight back.

"What on earth d'you think you're doing?" she roared at Pierre's set face.

"You go too far when you allow yourself to be kissed like that by your ex-lovers!" he shouted back at her.

She was stunned. She stared up at his white face for a long moment and then she clenched both her fists, preparing to do battle.

"Oh? And what that's to do with you?" she demanded.

"This," he said shortly, and he was kissing her himself. It hurt because he was as angry as she was, but even so, she wasn't at all certain that it wasn't one of the most wonderful moments of her life.

Chapter Eight

"*Let me go!*" She spoke in English, a sure sign of her agitation.

"So that you can go back to *entertaining* your Jean-Louis?"

"He's not mine!"

Too late she saw she might have done better to deny the rest of his accusation first.

"Isn't he?" Pierre said grimly. "He behaves as if he were."

"That's hardly my fault," Stephanie claimed. "I didn't invite him here!" She was annoyed to hear that she sounded on the defensive. She *felt* on the defensive! She rubbed her arms where he had been holding her. "What's it got to do with you anyway?" she demanded. "You're not my keeper!"

"I thought you could do with some help," he said,

somewhat smugly. "It's best to be ruthless when you're giving someone their marching orders, not kiss them goodbye."

Stephanie glared at him. "I suppose it didn't occur to you to mind your own business?"

"If you're an Anders, you are my business."

"Still afraid that I'm going to take advantage of Grandmère?" she mocked him.

"Or that they may take advantage of you."

How could they? Her mockery grew deeper. The Anders didn't know her. All the time they'd been here they'd hardly acknowledged her existence. What could they do to her?

"They're not interested in me," she said positively.

"Oh? How did Jean-Louis know you're here?"

"Mother sent him." She said it on a sigh, reflecting that her mother was going to be disappointed that she hadn't managed to bring about a grand reconciliation. Whatever her stepfather had thought of him, her mother had always had a soft spot for Jean-Louis. He was socially acceptable, with the beautiful manners of his profession, at least where older women were concerned, and he earned a lot of money. Mrs. Ironside was a great believer that while romance was fine, to be comfortable was far, far better. Romance wore off, she had frequently told her daughter, and, although misery didn't invariably follow, it was a great deal more satisfying for a woman to be miserable and rich than to be miserable and not know where the next penny was coming from. "She probably thought I was still in love with him."

"Didn't you tell her he'd only dazzled you for a while?"

Stephanie was shocked. "Certainly not. And who told you that?"

His smile made her blush. "Why, you did," he said.

She remembered that she had. "Oh well," she dismissed it, "I found he meant a lot less to me than I'd thought at one time. I guess I was lonely."

"Lonely? You?"

She was flattered that he didn't believe her. She wasn't sure she believed herself. It was ridiculous to have been lonely in a household where people were always coming and going at every hour of the day and night.

"Not really lonely," she said aloud.

He nodded his head in the direction of the dairy. "D'you want me to send him away?" he asked her.

"Of course not! *If* I want him to go, I'll ask him myself!"

"See that you do," he advised.

"Only if I want to!" she put in quickly.

Pierre sketched her a salute. "I'll be around if you need me." His voice softened, making her feel mushy and inclined to cry. "Better get it over with, *petite*, before he gets too fond of your new possessions and decides to take you along with them."

Stephanie manufactured a kind of indignation and was quite pleased with the results. "Jean-Louis isn't like that!" she denied.

Pierre grinned. "Are you sure?"

"He has enough of his own," she said.

"Unlike the Anders?"

She creased her brow. Were the Anders rich? She doubted it somehow. They'd all worn off-the-peg clothes, none of which had fitted very well, and all in that shiny, well-worn black that meant they were far from being new. Berthe's clothes had had the musty smell of being hidden away in a closet for too long. Stephanie wouldn't have been surprised to learn that both the women had bought their clothes in rummage sales, and thought that everyone else should save money by doing likewise. The picture of them rummaging through the loads of cast-off clothing that nobody else would buy made her want to laugh. There were lovely things to be bought at rummage sales, but those two wouldn't see them in their search for something 'suitable' and 'serviceable'. They wouldn't have been seen dead in the kind of thing Stephanie liked to buy, like old lace and the quality clothes of yesteryear.

"I think you ought to apologise to Jean-Louis," she said in a light, cool voice. "He'll be madder than a wet hen at being shut in the dairy like that."

"But not at my kissing you?"

Stephanie shrugged. "He knows I can take care of myself."

Pierre made a sound in the back of his throat that could have been a laugh. "The man's a fool!"

Stephanie twisted her lips into a smile. "For wanting me?"

He laughed out loud then. "For thinking you want him," he retorted.

"I'm not sure I don't."

"Then you're a bigger fool than he is!"

"I don't see why," she argued. "Mother won't rest until she gets me married off to someone, and why not him? He's madly suitable in a lot of ways."

"Except in the one way that matters."

She primped up her mouth and lifted her chin. "One can exaggerate the importance of that," she said wisely.

"You know all about it, of course?"

Probably not, she was honest enough to admit to herself, but she wasn't going to admit it to him. After all, she had never been short of boyfriends, though the accent had been more on the friend than anything else. She had never wanted anything more from them.

"I know enough," she said.

"Then apply that knowledge to getting rid of Jean-Louis, or I'll be tempted to take your education in hand myself!" he threatened.

"You can try!" she dared him.

She stepped away from him but she wasn't nearly quick enough. Perhaps she hadn't wanted to be. However it was, she felt a thrill of satisfaction as he brought her hard up against his body and looked down into her wide green eyes with a message that sent her blood racing through her veins.

A sound of knocking came from the dairy door, getting angrier all the time. "Jean-Louis!" she exclaimed. She was ashamed that for a second she had forgotten all about him. She released herself firmly, swallowing down the regret that washed through her body. "It's all your fault!" she added bitterly.

"I'll leave you to explain that to him," he agreed cheerfully.

He was gone when she looked up. It was as if the sun had gone in, but she wouldn't admit as much, not even to herself. What did she care about Pierre? What did she care about any of them? Certainly, she cared less than nothing for the increasingly violent-sounding Jean-Louis!

Jean-Louis exploded out of the dairy the second she released him. She stood back well out of the way, and watched him ricochet off the opposite wall.

"I'm sorry about that," she said. "Though I expect you understand it better than I do. I've never been able to understand the French sense of humour, as you know."

He grunted, unmollified by her bland expression. "I don't think it was meant to be funny," he said cautiously.

She raised her brows. "Why else would anyone want to lock you in?"

"I don't know," he admitted. "Not unless this Pierre has something going with you. Has he?"

"He's my grandmother's adopted son."

"Oh, I see." Jean-Louis brushed his hands together. "That's all right then. Let's get back to us!"

"There's nothing to get back to," Stephanie denied. "It was all over a long time ago between us. You were quite right when you said I would make an unsuitable wife for you. I would. Perhaps not for the reasons you gave, because they were just excuses to be rid of me, but because I don't love you and never did. I *like* you very much—"

"What's wrong with liking?"

"All the usual things," she smiled. "My heart doesn't go 'zing' when you kiss me—"

"Stephanie! Be serious!"

She looked at him, her green eyes hardening as she did so. "I am serious."

He saw that she was. "Look," he said, "supposing we start again. Perhaps I took too much for granted, walking in on you here without telling you beforehand and expecting you to fall into my arms. Your mother said you were hurt when I broke off our engagement. I didn't mean to hurt you, Stephanie, you've got to believe that!"

"I do."

"Well then, there's no point in going on punishing me, is there?"

"You didn't mean to hurt me, but you succeeded in telling me quite a lot about yourself. It was too bad if I were hurt. Your career came first and I came nowhere. When I marry, I want to come first with my husband. I'll never come first with you. I doubt if I'd figure in your list of top ten priorities, and that isn't good enough for me."

"You're being ridiculous," he began. "What list of priorities?"

She counted them off on her fingers. "Your career; money; position; what people think of you; your skills at manipulating people to do things your way; your persuasive tongue—"

"I thought you said you liked me!"

"I do!"

His eyes narrowed. "And do you also like this Pierre of yours?"

She didn't have to lie about it. She didn't like Pierre at all. All week she'd been persuading herself how much happier she was when he kept out of her way. She was glad Jean-Louis hadn't asked her another question, one she was still ducking from asking herself, one which she wouldn't even allow herself to formulate, in case the answer was as overwhelming as she suspected it might be.

"Not much!" She smiled a cheerful smile and shrugged her shoulders to show him how little she cared.

"You seemed to," Jean-Louis grunted. "I could hear you whispering together when I was locked in."

Stephanie felt on firmer ground. "Oh, hardly whispering! I was giving him a piece of my mind for manhandling me like that. He may be stronger than I am—and bigger—"

"I didn't think his type would appeal to you," Jean-Louis said with satisfaction.

Stephanie started. "Why not?"

Jean-Louis leered at her. "Too physical. The masterful type. You've never gone for that sort of thing."

And she never had! Never before! She'd made the best of being kissed by Jean-Louis but it had hardly mattered to her at all. On the other hand, Pierre had only to be in the same room with her for her to be overcome by his presence. The whole atmosphere changed. He was there in the air she breathed, as life-giving as the oxygen.

"You don't know me at all," she remarked aloud.

He was as complacent as ever. "Who knows you better? You've always had a multitude of friends, but if you told me you were other than the virgin girl I expect to marry, I shouldn't believe you!"

"Really?"

She wasn't annoyed. She wasn't anything very much. Jean-Louis had no power to move her even to anger. She kept telling herself that she liked him very much, and wondering how on earth she had managed to kid herself that she would be happy married to him. She had told Pierre she had been dazzled by him, now she could only think that she had dazzled herself by inventing someone quite different from the reality of this nice enough yet rather pompous man, who would bore her half to death if she had to see him often.

He smiled at her as though she were a difficult child. "Your family expects us to get together again too, Stephanie. The sooner we take the plunge the better everyone'll be pleased."

"Except me," Stephanie said.

His annoyance would have amused her under other circumstances. "Don't be ridiculous!" he bade her. "I'm going straight back to your grandmother now, whether you come with me or not, to tell her that we're going to be married as soon as all the arrangements can be made. I understand you may be nervous, even that you may want to punish me a little for the past, but I really can't allow—"

"Allow?" Stephanie repeated.

"My dear girl—"

"I'm not your dear anything. Tell Grandmère anything you please, but you'll only be making a fool of yourself. I'm not marrying you or anyone else!"

He looked at her as if he were seeing her for the first time. "You've always wanted to marry me!" he complained.

"Well, I don't any longer."

He reached out for her, not with affection but with anger, and dragged her up against him. "I'll soon change your mind!" he threatened. His arms were steel bands about her. She hadn't known he was so strong. At first, she allowed him to kiss her, but when he started pulling at her clothes she pushed away from him, uncaring any longer as to whether she would hurt his feelings by her rejection.

"Go away and leave me alone!" she ground out.

"When I'm good and ready, I'll think about it!"

He overcame her with an ease that dismayed her. She clenched her teeth together and forced herself to relax, hoping to catch him off his guard.

"A few kisses will change your mind. A display of reluctance is all very well, my dear, but a man needs something more from time to time. You can't pretend with me!"

Stephanie dug her elbows into his ribs and waited her opportunity to kick him on the shins. She hadn't expected much success, but to her surprise his hold slackened and she found herself free. Gasping at her victory, she raised her eyes from the floor to see what had happened to him. Her astonishment was complete when she saw her tormentor writhing in Pierre's half nelson, from which he had as little chance of escaping as she had had from him.

"What shall I do with him?" Pierre asked her cheerfully.

"Let him go! *Must* you interfere all the time?"

"Ah now," said Pierre, "that reminds me I have something to say to you, Stephanie Ironside Anders, and now is as good as any other time. I'll return this to your grandmother's keeping and then you are coming with me, so don't go away!" His smile was as amiable as his tone of voice. Even so, Stephanie didn't dare say anything at all.

She watched in silence as the two men disappeared. "I'm going to marry her!" she could hear Jean-Louis complaining, and Pierre's reassuring growl of an answer, which could have been anything at all.

Left alone, Stephanie wondered if she should take her opportunity to get away from them both. There was probably a bus to Rouen—or to Lisieux—but she wasn't even packed. Besides, it seemed shabby to run away without a word to her grandmother. Not for the first time, Stephanie wished she'd been brought up to be as mannerless as some others of her generation. As it was, it seemed she had no choice but wait for Pierre's return. She forgot the instant where she had been genuinely frightened as she wrestled with Jean-Louis. She forgot everything but Pierre's irritating habit of sticking his nose in where it was not wanted. She'd wait, she decided, but not because he wanted her to; she'd wait because she had something to say to him about the way he seemed to think that he could get away with anything he did around her. Why didn't he go to his own house and worry about his own affairs—of which she was sure he had many!

By the time he came back to the dairy she was in a towering rage, partly with herself for getting into this ridiculous position, but mostly with him because the last thing she wanted was to have to feel grateful to him!

"Ready?" he asked her.

She shook her head. "I'm not going anywhere with you!" she declared.

"No?" His dark eyes filled with amusement. "Would you rather go with Jean-Louis?"

"The trouble with men is that they never stop to ask!" she stormed at him. "Why should I want to go with either of you?"

"That's what I want to talk to you about."

She wished he were a little less certain of himself, or that she had more faith in her own abilities to cope with him. No matter how determined she was inside, she only had to look at him to want something quite different. She had developed a split personality, with her body clamouring for one thing and her mind for another.

She lifted her chin. "I don't want to talk to you!"

"You will."

Excitement nibbled at her resolution. She wanted to go with him, however much she might pretend otherwise.

"The only thing I have to say is goodbye," she brought out. "I have to be in Rouen tomorrow—"

"You're going with him!"

She opened her eyes wide, her face the picture of innocence. "With Jean-Louis?"

"Whom else would you be going with?"

Her answer was as flippant as she felt the question to be. "Do I have a choice?"

She couldn't meet his eyes. There was a look in them that melted her inside and frightened her half to death. She couldn't give up her will power to a stranger. She had to retain her independence. She had to remember that he was still suspicious of her motives for allowing herself to be brought here in the first place. He wasn't a friend, more probably a foe, but she was uneasily aware that if he wanted it that way he would probably end up her lover.

"Yes, you have a choice," he bit out. "You can come with me."

She blinked. "To Rouen?"

"Don't be stupid, Stephanie!"

She took a deep breath. "Why would you want to take me anywhere else?"

"Come with me and find out!"

He held out his hand to her, and she put her own into it before she had time to think. Far from giving way, she ought to take to her heels and run as far and as fast as she could in the opposite direction.

"Where are we going?"

"To my house. I'll make you an English cup of tea and then we'll talk."

She licked her lips, enjoying the knowledge that she had no intention of resisting the temptation this man offered her.

"And then what?" she almost whispered.

A muscle jerked in his cheek, but whether it was amusement or not she couldn't tell. "If you succeed in persuading me that's what you really want to do, I'll drive you to Rouen," he said.

She dropped her eyes to the top button on his shirt. She almost answered him, "Rouen? Where's Rouen?" But she didn't quite dare. If she had said that, or something similar, he would have known that she wasn't crazy about going to Rouen at all. Her ambitions to be the leading artist of her generation seemed to have been left on the other side of the great divide that was her discovery that she was a different person to the one she had always thought herself to be. She had seen herself as sensible, fun-loving, friendly, and, above everything else, cool. She didn't feel cool now. She felt like an electric storm, the lightning licking through her veins and the rumbles of thunder being the sound of her heart as it beat against her ribs in anticipation.

"Perhaps I'll paint a portrait of you instead," she said aloud.

"To go with the one of your father?"

She still wouldn't look at him. She didn't need to see him to sense his slightest mood change, or anything else about him.

"I still haven't seen that," she said. "What kind of a portrait is it? Does it show simply what he looked like, or the inner man?"

"A bit of both, I should imagine."

"I wonder what colour his eyes were," she mused aloud. It would be hard to recapture the exact shade of Pierre's. They changed with his thoughts. When he had kissed her. . . .

"Not as green as yours and your grandmother's," he answered her. "Or so she told me. It's unusual to have eyes as green as yours."

There was no sign of his car, so she supposed he had walked over earlier that day. Should she change her shoes for others more suited to the task of crossing the fields that lay between the two houses? He gave her no opportunity to suggest such a thing. His hand tightened on hers as if he suspected her of trying to get away from him after all. She moved her forefinger against the palm of his hand in a gesture of reassurance and was surprised to see a slight flush mount from his neck into his face.

"You make me as uncertain as a young man on his first date," he confessed, smiling at her.

"I hope not!" she retorted.

"Don't you want me to kiss you?"

She pretended to think about it. "Uh-huh, but not the quick fumble of a first date," she teased him.

"I think I can guarantee something better than that," he answered.

"I'm sure you can!"

His smile was bland. "Jealous?"

"Certainly not!" she denied.

"Your eyes are green," he reminded her.

"But not with envy of your loves."

He raised his brows in enquiry, but she couldn't bring herself to continue the thought as it had occurred to her. She couldn't be envious of *them*, because she was here and they were not.

"They're still green," he said.

She shrugged her shoulders. "I was thinking of Jean-Louis, and marriage, and my career, things like that."

"I don't think your career means much to you," he commented.

It was all too true! "Tell me about your career," she commanded. "Tell me about William the Conqueror —the man, not the king."

"He married Mathilda of Flanders. She was a widow who thought herself too good for the bastard William. He paid her out for her insults by calling on her in his father's castle and delivering a sound beating by way of reply. It was an unusual match in those days—a love match, by all accounts."

Stephanie gave up the unequal battle and bent down to remove her shoes, scuffing her bare feet in the grass with a sensuous pleasure that was new to her.

"It sounds a drastic way of wooing a wife," she said.

"Proof positive that it doesn't do to drive a Norman too far," he agreed dryly.

Her breath caught in the back of her throat. "Are Normans given to violence?"

He took her shoes from her and gave her a small push along the beaten track that led to his house.

"You're going the right way about finding out," he said.

Chapter Nine

His house was every bit as delightful as she had remembered it from her previous visit. She had thought she might have built up its charms in her mind, feeling vaguely disloyal to her grandmother and the house where she was staying because of her strong preference. But she hadn't. Pierre's house was her favourite every time.

She sighed as she sipped her tea. "I should be getting back. My grandmother'll think I have no manners at all."

Pierre watched her closely. "She'll know where you are."

"That's not the point." She put her cup and saucer down with resolution, getting to her feet. "The point is that I'm her guest, not yours, and she's expecting me back for lunch. It was my mother who sent Jean-Louis here."

"And you can't wait to get back to him?"

She thought she'd taken enough aggravation from Pierre for one day. She'd been disappointed when he'd done no more than make her a cup of tea after their arrival. She didn't know what she'd been expecting, but it hadn't been that! She might as well have stayed close by her grandmother's side, and not set up this conflict between what she wanted to do and what she knew would be better for her in the long run.

"I owe him something," she said aloud, fishing for her shoes from under the sofa. "He's an old friend."

Pierre's hands were on her shoulders, hauling her to her feet and turning her round to face him.

"And what else is he?" he demanded.

What else? Very little, she hoped. Stephanie shut her mouth in a determined line. "That's my business!" she snapped. "It's got nothing to do with you!"

"I'm making it my business!"

She shrugged. "Too bad."

He shook her, not hard, but hard enough to warn her that he was restraining himself only with difficulty. She caught a glimpse of the dark fire in his eyes and hastily lowered her own before he could ignite her very short fuse. It was unfair that any man should be so attractive to her—especially as his interest in her was strictly a family matter, or maybe a passing fancy. She thought he did fancy her, but he wouldn't want to go too far, knowing her to be her grandmother's granddaughter as he did. And *that* ought to be a matter for rejoicing, not regret, she chided herself, recognising that the shivering excitement inside her was as unreliable as its progenitor.

He bent his head towards hers. "You're too much a woman to settle for Jean-Louis—"

"You know nothing about him!" she claimed wildly.

"I know quite a lot about you!"

"Not as much as you think!" She put up her hands and pushed him away from her, hating herself for wanting to do the reverse.

He held his hands up in mock surrender. "We haven't had our talk yet, Stephanie. After accepting my tea, don't you think you owe me a hearing?"

She was cautious, not trusting him, and herself even less. "Make it quick!"

He sat down on the sofa and patted the cushion beside him for her to do likewise. Stephanie went and sat on a chair on the other side of the room, putting on her shoes to give herself something to do with her hands before they betrayed her lack of assurance to someone other than herself.

"Did you know Tante Janine and your mother quarrelled after your father's death?"

Stephanie shook her head. "It wouldn't have been my mother's fault. She never quarrels with anyone," she said.

Pierre shut his eyes briefly. "It doesn't matter whose fault it was, it was the reason why Tante Janine lost touch with you. She, at least, has regretted it all these years. Think about it, Stephanie. It won't hurt anyone for you to stay and be her granddaughter for a while, will it?"

"I have my own life to live—"

"She'll make it up to you," he urged her. "It needn't be for long."

"I have to be in Rouen tomorrow!"

He hesitated. "How serious are you about your career?"

"I'm serious about wanting to paint." She couldn't honestly say it was more than that. Her stepfather had left her enough money to live on if she was even halfway careful, but he had also insisted she should make a push to do something off her own bat, to justify her existence, as he had put it. Stephanie had wanted to paint for as long as she could remember, but she also knew that the openings in commercial art for someone like herself were limited. She had talent —more than most—but the kind of paintings she wanted to do were not the kind which was fashionable in advertising today. She had thought she might design materials.

"Why Rouen?"

"Oh, need you ask? Next to Paris, Rouen's the place where I most want to study. I can learn so much there. They may be able to teach me to channel my work into more commercial lines. I *need* time there before I start work for myself in England."

"Tante Janine needs your time more."

She didn't want to listen to him. "I can visit from Rouen."

"Will you?"

Knowing Pierre was here, it'd be hard to stay away. She set her mouth into a tight line and refused to look at him.

"I'm going to ask Jean-Louis to give me a lift to Rouen—"

"You'd go all that way alone with him?"

She hunched her shoulders. "Why not? He's not a monster! I've known him for years. It'll give me time to explain to him why I'm not going to marry him. Besides, I *like* Jean-Louis! I always have!"

"That isn't what he's looking for from you—"

"Yes, well, it's nothing to do with you, is it?" Stephanie asserted herself. "That's between me and him. I can handle Jean-Louis."

It was Pierre that she couldn't handle. He was a much more real danger than the luckless Jean-Louis!

Pierre stood up as she did, crossing the room with a speed that deprived her of any avenue for escape.

"You're not going anywhere with him!" he shot at her. She could feel the impact of his words somewhere in the region of her ribs and realised that it had to be fantasy. It was the painful pressure of his fingers. "Stay here with us!"

"I can't!" She'd meant to sound determined and in control of herself, her own mistress, well able to make her own decisions. She wasn't going to turn her back on her grandmother, but she had every right to pursue her own life. A couple of months ago she hadn't known who she was, let alone that she had a grandmother in France, with eyes as green as her own, and a dignity that Stephanie hoped she would learn to achieve one day.

"Then don't go with Jean-Louis!"

"It doesn't matter who I go with—"

"It matters to me!"

Of course he didn't mean that! She knew better! She wished she could have laughed it off as lightly as it deserved, but she felt more like crying than laughing. If things had been different—but what was the use of wishing for the moon? Things were not different. Pierre might enjoy kissing her and flirting with her a little, but he hadn't shown any sign of wanting her to stay because she was the person she was. She had to remember that. To Pierre, she was first and foremost his beloved Tante Janine's granddaughter, nothing more.

She pulled away from him. "I'd better get back—"

"I'm coming with you! Tante Janine'll soon put a stop to your going with Jean-Louis!"

"She won't, you know."

The words were quietly spoken but they were deeply meant. She couldn't afford to allow her grandmother to think she could run her whole life. It might be the custom in France for the older generation to demand and receive an obedience from the young that was unknown now in Britain, but she couldn't allow it for herself. She was used to having her independence. Her stepfather had always encouraged her to make her own decisions. Her lips twisted in memory of how bitterly he had disliked the idea of her marrying Jean-Louis, and yet he had never once suggested she should change her mind to please him.

"If you're unhappy with him, don't be afraid to come back," he had said. Her mother had added, "Love can hurt, but not loving hurts a great deal more." Stephanie hadn't really listened to either of them, but she remembered what they had said now, and it made sense. She didn't love Jean-Louis, so she wasn't going to marry him. As for Pierre—she wouldn't think about Pierre at all if she could help it.

That was easier said than done when he was standing so close to her that she felt they were breathing the same air. She could breathe him in and imagine—her eyes opened wide. It wasn't her imagination that he was unbuttoning her bodice as she stood there.

"Pierre!" she gasped.

"We haven't finished talking yet," he muttered.

"D'you call that talking?"

"There are more ways of communicating than with words. You don't listen when I talk to you, but I'm a resourceful man, *ma petite,* I'll find some way of keeping you here."

"That's what you think!"

He came closer still despite her efforts to wriggle free. "I have to attract your attention somehow."

If she gave in a little bit, she might lose the immediate battle, but she was still sure she'd win the war. She relaxed against him, buttoning up her bodice as fast as he undid it.

"Not that way," she said. "I'll have to know you better before I'll agree to undress for you."

His eyes lit with amusement. "How much better?"

She put her head on one side, considering the matter. "Much better than I know you now. We can work on it whenever I come to visit my grandmother."

"I've a better idea than that. Why don't we work on it now?"

She shook her head. "I'm going to Rouen with Jean-Louis now. You're the one who doesn't listen—"

His lips explored hers with a gentleness that beguiled her into thinking she could end it whenever she wished. She strained closer to him, running her fingers through his thick, dark hair. It was bliss. She forgot how much it mattered to her to leave at once for Rouen. She forgot everything except the burning desire that swept through her like a tidal wave, demolishing her defences with ease.

"Pierre, I've got to go—"

"You've got to stay here, with me," he answered with mounting satisfaction. "We both know it. We want each other too much for you to go running off anywhere right now."

Wanting wasn't loving! The words screamed through her mind just as his mouth took command of hers. When his tongue met hers, she thought she was already addicted to the taste of him. He filled her five senses with his presence, making her forget everything else. The only difference was that she loved him as well as wanting him, whereas his was a passing need that would be forgotten as soon as it was indulged.

"Please, Pierre, let me go!"

"I can't! *Madone,* don't ask me to now!"

She didn't recognise the endearment, but she suspected it had little to do with love. She was being torn in two, half by her longing to give herself to him, half by the pain of being offered lust in the place of love.

"Wanting isn't enough," she said slowly.

He let her go, pushing her away from him with such violence that she nearly fell. "What else is there?" he flung at her. "My God, you're prepared to settle for marriage with Jean-Louis, feeling nothing for him. Why, when you have all that matters with me?"

"Sex isn't everything," she answered with as much dignity as she could.

"It can seem like everything if you're fool enough to marry without it!"

"Anyway," she protested, "How d'you know I haven't got it with Jean-Louis?"

He groaned out loud. "Get out of here while you still can," he advised her. "Get out and help Tante Janine with her lunch guest if you must, but don't go anywhere with him, Stephanie Ironside Anders, not if you value your pretty little neck."

A new emotion snagged her breath, an emotion she recognised as fear. She stiffened her backbone and glared at her tormentor.

"I'm going! And I'd advise you to mind your own business—"

"That's what I intend to do."

His voice was like shiny steel and she suspected he could be just as deadly.

"Good, because if there's one thing I can't stand it's being told what to do by arrogant males such as yourself!"

"Indeed?"

"Yes, *indeed!*"

"Pity, because I'm making you my business as, in your heart, you've known for a long time now. If you try to go anywhere with Jean-Louis, I'll come after you, my sweet, and I'll drag you back by your hair, which I'll enjoy a great deal more than you will!"

She stared at him, turning over in her mind the various retorts she might have made. None of them seemed adequate to the occasion. She could tell him she didn't believe him—and she was almost sure she didn't—but she couldn't quite summon up the necessary courage to call his bluff. Then she might have told him how much she despised men who went in for the caveman technique of threatening women with physical violence, but she wasn't really afraid that he'd ever hurt her—not that way!

She licked her lips. "I have to be in Rouen tomorrow."

He pointed towards the telephone. "Be my guest," he invited her. "Tell them you can't make it. Tell them you've got some growing up to do before you can spare the time to do any real work with them—"

"It's you who's being childish about this!" she exclaimed infuriated.

"Because I know what I want?"

"Because you think that what you want is the only thing that matters!" she retorted.

His glance was imperturbable, a complete contrast to the turmoil that was going on inside her. Somehow that made her more furious than ever.

"Where you're concerned, it is," he said, and smiled at her, patting her scarlet cheek with a comforting hand. "Don't be tempted to pick up the challenge, will you? I mean every word of it. I'll do whatever it takes to keep you safely with Tante Janine for the next few weeks. She needs you."

Stephanie felt as if a pit had opened up in front of her feet and she had very nearly walked into it. *She* didn't matter to him at all! He was doing all this for his precious Tante Janine! Probably he had even kissed her with that in mind. She knew now what the term heartbreak meant. It meant coming apart at the seams and not being able to put oneself together again.

"I'll do as I think best," she said, wondering if she sounded as cold as she felt inside.

She didn't remember afterwards how she had got outside. She walked away from the house as if in a dream, and was genuinely startled when Pierre came after her, his expression wry.

"I'll drive you back," he offered.

"I'd sooner walk!"

"And be late for lunch?"

"I'm not going anywhere with you!"

He opened the door of the car. "Get in!"

It was not the moment to be indecisive. Nobody knew that better than she. She looked at the car and she thought about the rough track over which they had come. She didn't really feel like walking back that way in her bare feet, and her shoes hurt when she walked further than a few yards in them. With an elaborate sigh she got into the passenger seat, averting her face so that he wouldn't see her defeated look.

"Did I say something to offend you?" Pierre asked as he got in beside her.

"No."

His speculative glance made her feel guilty. He had been brought up by her grandmother and owed her a great deal. Was it so surprising that for him her needs and happiness came before everyone else's? If she, Stephanie, had misunderstood him somewhere along the way, it was her own fault. Like any other French-man, he'd used his kisses to sweeten the pill. Well, she'd always known what Frenchmen were like! Why should she be surprised at that?

"Worried about Jean-Louis?" he went on.

"Of course not!"

"Then you should be," he came back swiftly.

"Jean-Louis is an old friend—"

Pierre started up the car. "He's never been a friend of yours and never will be. It beats me why some women seem to have no more ambition in life than to be turned into a mirror for some man to polish his image in front of!"

He sounded angry, which surprised her. Yet it was an apt enough description of Jean-Louis, she thought with an inward smile, but not of her! She was no man's looking glass and never would be!

"I thought that that was what you wanted from me," she said dryly. "Women with careers of their own can afford to be much more independent than most men—most *Frenchmen*—would like them to be!"

He looked positively smug. "Ah, so that's what you hold against me? Frenchmen are not all tarred by the same brush, my love. Think of me as a Norman and you'll like me a whole lot better."

"The Normans are the worst of the lot!" she claimed wildly. "Look at your William. He couldn't bear it when Mathilda told him the truth—oh no! He wasn't happy until he'd reduced her to being as sycophantic as everyone else about him! I'll bet she still thought of him as a bastard until his dying day!"

Pierre put back his head and laughed. "Better to have a man for your husband than a gentleman, if you have to choose between the two," he teased her. "Jean-Louis is far too gentlemanly to be of much use to you between the sheets!"

Stephanie was unaccustomed to such blunt speech. She would have liked to have asked him if he thought he could do any better, but wisely changed her mind in the nick of time. Instead, she gave him a wide-eyed, innocent look and said sweetly, "Well, that's hardly your worry, is it?"

He flashed her a look of such brooding male power that she wilted in the face of it. "Nor will it be yours, *mignonne,* I promise you that!"

She was thankful that they'd arrived outside her grandmother's house and that she wasn't called on for an answer. She shot out of the car as if Nemesis was brandishing a sword over her head, and ran for the safety of the house. She would not allow him to get to her ever again. She would not! Surely, somewhere inside her, she could find enough pride to demolish the challenge of a mere Norman? Mathilda hadn't managed it. She knew that from the way Pierre had laughed at her hopeful comment that Mathilda had thought of her Norman as a bastard until the day of his death. Why should Mathilda have cared? The word probably hadn't acquired its double meaning at that time. Blast William, and blast Pierre! He had got under her skin so thoroughly that she didn't think she'd ever be free of him again.

Her grandmother was waiting for her in the salon. Stephanie looked round for Jean-Louis, but he wasn't there.

"Where've you been, child?" her grandmother greeted her.

"With Pierre. Has Jean-Louis gone?"

Her grandmother pulled down her upper lip in a contemptuous gesture. "That one isn't for you," she said grandly.

Stephanie smothered a laugh that bordered on the hysterical. "I could've told you that!"

"It's a pity you didn't tell your mother and save us all a deal of trouble," her grandmother chided her.

"I did tell her it wasn't the end of the world when he broke off our engagement. She wasn't listening. Jean-Louis has a great deal of money—"

She saw the sympathy in her grandmother's eyes and wanted to explain that her mother had only wanted the best for her, but, having been hurt by love herself, she had thought in terms of material security before all else.

"Where is Jean-Louis?" she asked sharply.

"He went to wash his hands before lunch. He wasn't pleased at being left to his own devices all morning. I'd thought you'd better manners—"

"Blame Pierre!"

"Ah!"

Stephanie turned baleful eyes on the old lady. "Now, what d'you mean by that?" she demanded.

"Nothing, nothing at all," Madame Anders denied. A smile appeared in the back of the green eyes which were so like her granddaughter's. "He seems to enjoy kidnapping you when he has nothing better to do," she remarked. "Is he jealous of Jean-Louis?"

"He wouldn't have any reason to be," Stephanie pointed out.

"Jean-Louis thinks he has."

Stephanie shrugged. "Jean-Louis knows it's all over

between us. He may have hoped for a moment when
Mother got in touch with him, but it wasn't because of
any feeling he has for me. I expect Mother hinted I'd
come into a fortune from my *French* family. Once he's
found a good reason to let his pride off the hook he'll
be relieved to be shot of the whole affair. Jean-Louis
was never in love with me—or I with him."

Her grandmother chuckled. "You didn't think that
when you got engaged to him. Who's been teaching
you about love, *ma mie?*"

"One can't help growing up—"

"Are you sure it has nothing to do with Pierre?"

"Nothing at all!"

"I hope you're right," her grandmother murmured.
"Pierre's like a bear with a sore head when he's
thwarted. If he had to kidnap you a third time it might
be a rather uncomfortable experience for you."

Stephanie forced a smile. "He's only worrying
about you. He doesn't understand I have a life of my
own. Grandmère I'll come back whenever I can, but I
must take up my place at Rouen. If I miss it, I might
as well say goodbye to my whole career. You do
understand, don't you?"

"This career means so much to you?"

Stephanie nodded. "My stepfather left me enough
to live on if I'm careful, but I want to be someone in
my own right, too."

"Quite right. So you're off to Rouen—"

"With Jean-Louis, if he's going that way. Public
transport is as bad in France as it is in England."

Her grandmother pursed up her lips. "Have you
told Pierre?" she asked blandly.

Stephanie blushed. "I spent the whole morning telling him," she said.

Stephanie closed her suitcase with a snap. There was only one thing more she wanted to do before she left, and although she hadn't asked her grandmother's permission, she didn't think she'd mind. She glanced at herself in the mirror and surprised a dampness in her green eyes. If she were to cry now, she'd never stop! She smiled wryly at herself. Jean-Louis had been delighted when she had asked him to drive her to Rouen. With surprising perspicacity he'd taken her request for what it was, a plea for help.

"Pierre getting too much for you?" he had asked.

"He's only a family connection—"

"You're right, of course," Jean-Louis had added, and she had known in that moment how much he had always secretly despised her. "He'd make demands on you you couldn't begin to answer. He's too physical by half for a sweet little thing like you. You could have done much better with me. I wouldn't have frightened you half to death!"

No, she'd have been bored to death instead!

Stephanie's smile deepened, but she wasn't bluffing herself. She could see the telltale signs of strain at the corners of her eyes and was tempted to change her mind and stay after all. Pierre—she would *not* think about Pierre, not under any circumstances. If she did she'd break down and cry in earnest and then everyone would know. . . .

She straightened her shoulders and tossed her head with a jaunty air. Her grandmother's bedroom door was open and she only had to push it further ajar to walk inside. Her eyes flew to the portrait of her father and she went and stood beneath it, looking up at him and wondering what life would have been like had he come home from the war in Algeria. He looked familiar and yet a complete stranger to her. She had no feelings about him at all, though she suspected he provided the answers to many questions that she had regarding her mother.

"She loved you," she told him. He stared blankly back at her. Stephanie looked away and her eyes fell on a photo beside the bed, a photo of Pierre. "And I love him," she added under her breath. "Only he's not going to freeze me over for all time, as losing you did to Mother. I'm going to live, and love—and lose, and start all over again! You see if I don't."

But she knew it as a lie even as she spoke the words. Like her mother before her, there was only one man who could make her come alive in that one particular way. The difference was that she wouldn't settle for second best with another man. Then she laughed. Poor Jean-Louis would never forgive her if he were to find out that she preferred single misery to wedded bliss with him. She would devote her life to her art, and if fame and fortune were a poor recompense for what might have been if Pierre had loved her, it was a great deal better than anything else she could think of.

Chapter Ten

"What am I to tell Pierre?"

Stephanie looked helplessly at her grandmother. "You don't have to tell him anything. He'll know where I am."

Madame Anders sighed. "You're like your mother —stubborn!" she said.

Stephanie smiled. "Will you miss me?" she said, trying to introduce a lighter note.

"I missed your mother, too."

"She had nothing to stay for. I expect she was homesick—"

"She said she was too young to be a widow."

Stephanie could understand that. "She wasn't very old, was she?" she said gently. "And she had me to consider. She probably didn't want to bring me up in a foreign country."

"France," the old lady said grandly, "is not a foreign country."

"It is to foreigners like me."

Her grandmother looked down her nose, thoroughly annoyed. "Since when are you a foreigner? Didn't we do everything to make your mother feel at home? Didn't we guard her night and day? And when Guy was gone, didn't we include her in all our plans? She didn't think about us at all—"

"You suffocated her!"

The two women looked at each other, equally appalled. "We did what we felt was best for her. After a proper period of mourning, we'd have looked round for a suitable husband for her and stepfather for you. She was like a daughter to us."

"The English have always valued their freedom. Didn't you think she'd want to choose her own husband?"

Madame Anders shrugged. "There's no harm in keeping unsuitable men away, is there? Naturally she would have had a choice—"

"Would she? You'd really like to do the same to me, Grandmère, wouldn't you? Find me a nice, steady Norman who lives not too far away, who'd guard and protect me for the rest of my days. Isn't that what you'd like for me?"

Her grandmother shrugged again. She wasn't enjoying this conversation, but she could think of no way of bringing it to an end. Stephanie could read her like a book.

"One has to be practical about such things," the older woman murmured at last. "Marriages should strengthen families, not tear them apart. It's good to unite old friends. Nowadays, it may be fashionable to pretend that girls are boys and can have the same freedoms, but it's the girls who'll suffer once they're women, with broken marriages, fatherless children and financial worries. But do they think of such things when they're young? What else are parents for but to guard them from such disasters?"

Stephanie sat on the floor at her grandmother's knee. "Didn't you trust my mother to do the right thing by herself?"

"The temptations—you wouldn't understand!"

Oh, wouldn't she? Stephanie had only to think of how she melted inside at the sound of Pierre's voice to know what temptations could lie in store for the unwary.

"I'm not considering marriage with anyone," she said aloud. "And if I don't marry, I need a secure career. That's why I'm going to Rouen today. I'll keep coming back though, if only to put our horrible relations in their place from time to time!"

Her grandmother thought what a pretty picture she made. She, herself, thought it ridiculous for any woman to claim she preferred to be on her own, especially if she were young and pretty. It would be terrible if it were to be some scruffy artist who introduced her to love. Artists could be quite respectable these days, or so she was told, but what would his parents be like? Dearly as she'd loved her husband, his relatives had left a lot to be desired—she despised the lot of them—but, until recently, she'd had her own family to help her cope with them. She didn't want to think of Stephanie battling with her in-laws all alone. Perhaps her mother had fallen on her feet, but it wasn't always like that. Far from it.

"What d'you think of Pierre?"

Stephanie was caught unawares. Before she had time to school her expression, a little of the misery inside escaped to reveal itself to the eagle eyes of the older woman.

"He's very fond of you," Stephanie said slowly.

"Too fond, perhaps?"

"Oh no! He ought to put you first—"

"Until he finds a woman of his own. I hope always to have a corner of his heart—"

"It'll be a very large corner," Stephanie told her, trying to keep the bitterness out of her voice.

"You sound as though you think his wife might resent that?" Madame Anders challenged her smoothly.

"Not if she came first. She might resent it if she found herself to be no more than a gift-wrapped package intended for you and not a person in her own right at all."

"Ah! So that's why you're running away! Oh well, Pierre will look after his own! What a good thing Jean-Louis will take you, *n'est-ce pas?* That should produce a reaction from Pierre! I wondered why you were punishing him by running off. I even thought that perhaps you'd found you couldn't love him after all, but it turns out to be a ridiculous muddle between the two of you, nothing more than that!"

"He wants to keep me here for your sake," Stephanie sighed.

Her grandmother cackled with laughter. "Fond of me he is, but not that fond, *ma chère!*"

Stephanie didn't press the point. If she were to tell her grandmother exactly what had taken place between Pierre and herself she would very likely cry, and that was the last thing she wanted to do. She might as well go out on a high note, she thought. Jean-Louis would lend her a certain cover, and if Pierre saw that as some kind of challenge, she really couldn't care less.

"I must go. Jean-Louis'll be waiting."

A momentary anxiety crossed her grandmother's features. "He understands that all's at an end between you?"

"He will by the time we get to Rouen," Stephanie promised.

Her grandmother nodded. "Be careful what you say to him. We know nothing about him—"

"Grandmère!"

"Did your mother make the necessary enquiries? She didn't tell me."

Stephanie bowed to the inevitable. "I don't know if she did or not, but believe me, I can cope with Jean-Louis."

"We must hope so."

Jean-Louis was polishing the immaculate paintwork on his car when Stephanie joined him. He finished what he was doing, stood back and admired his handiwork, and when he spoke to her, it was over his shoulder.

"I'm glad you've seen sense at last! Put your suitcase on the back seat and we'll be off."

Stephanie did as she was told. "Were you going to Rouen anyway?" she asked him, frowning as she did up her seatbelt.

"I was going to Paris, but I'd much rather go to Rouen with you! You know, darling, you've grown up a lot since I last saw you. You wouldn't have gone off with a man in the old days, let alone have suggested it!"

"I hadn't realised that that was what I'm doing now," Stephanie informed him. "I said I wanted a lift to Rouen and that's exactly what I want, nothing more!"

"It doesn't matter," he assured her. "I'm not in the least shocked. We'll be married later on, long before anyone else gets to hear about it, and you'll have your romantic memory to keep you warm in your old age."

Stephanie couldn't believe her ears. "I'm not going to marry you! Nor am I going to spend a weekend with you! If that's what you have in mind you can take me straight back to my grandmother!"

He patted her knee, a familiarity that set her teeth on edge. "Now, now, I've told you I don't think any less of you—"

"Jean-Louis, will you listen to me! I'm not going to marry you. I'm not going to make love with you. I don't love you and I never will. Now, are you going to give me a lift to Rouen, with no strings attached, or not?"

His jaw sagged and he missed the gear, making her want to laugh.

"But I thought—"

Stephanie breathed out. "You didn't think at all,

you took it for granted, just as you've always taken *me* for granted. You'll be much happier when you've got used to the idea though. You never really wanted to marry me in the first place, did you?"

"Of course I did!"

"Oh, Jean-Louis, tell the truth for once. I was there, I was suitable and my stepfather had a lot of money. There wasn't anything else there, was there?"

Jean-Louis gave her a sulky look. "You didn't seem to mind at the time," he pointed out.

"No, but as you've said, I've grown up a lot since then—"

"You mean someone made you grow up! It could've been me you know. I may not have been madly in love with you, but I wouldn't have minded teaching you this and that. I rather fancied the task, to tell you the truth."

"Just so long as you've given up any idea of being my tutor now," she murmured.

He was silent for so long that she thought he was going to lapse into one of his famous sulks, when he sometimes didn't speak to anyone for days together. Then he burst out, "It's that adopted son of your grandmother's isn't it? I never would have believed it! You could've had an easy life with me—"

"In a way," Stephanie agreed demurely. "My mother had an easy life with my stepfather."

"She was happy with him, wasn't she?"

"She was content."

"What's the difference?"

Stephanie shut her eyes, conjuring up the portrait of her father. "She was happy with Guy Anders," she said aloud. "I don't think she's ever really got over his death. I know she couldn't bear life in France without him. It had been *his* home before he died; after he was gone, it was a foreign land like any other."

"It's different for your mother. She's a sophisticated woman who knows about life. She knew what she was doing when she married again."

"I hope so," Stephanie said. "I hope they both did."

Jean-Louis jutted out his lower lip. "At least her Guy married her; Pierre will never marry you! He'll soon find out he doesn't have to. You realise that, don't you? Men like that are all the same! Beats me what women see in them. If you did marry him, you'd never be able to call your soul your own."

"Would I have been able to with you?" Stephanie asked, genuinely interested.

"We'd have had our arguments, I suppose, but we'd have decided them on equal terms. I wouldn't have taken you to bed to get my own way, but I wouldn't put it past him to think a few kisses are as good an argument as any when it comes to dealing with a woman."

Stephanie wouldn't put it past him either. What else had he been doing when he'd used the physical attraction between them to get her to stay longer with her grandmother?

She put a hand on Jean-Louis' arm. "Thank you for understanding," she said. "You're not hurt, are you?"

"No, but only because I haven't given up yet. A few weeks fending for yourself in Rouen and life with me might seem a whole lot more attractive to you. Your mother's on my side in that! Between us, we'll soon bring you over to our way of thinking."

"Ever the diplomat!" Stephanie teased him. "Give a little and hope to get back a lot?"

"You'll soon get tired of painting in a garret. I can wait."

"And Pierre?"

"I don't admire your taste. He may've done me a favour in a way. You've had your fling and you know it isn't going anywhere. You'll come back to me when you're good and ready."

"I see. You've got it all worked out?"

"I'm trained to work things out."

Stephanie tried not to smile. She hadn't dented his armour at all. He was as sure of himself as ever—and of her. And yet, he'd never really known her at all, or he would have known that she was a one-man woman like her mother. The only difference was that she was a lot younger, and the world had taken a turn or two since her father had been killed. Her mother wouldn't have felt comfortable on her own under any circumstances. Stephanie couldn't imagine herself contemplating another man for security; she knew there was none where there was no love to unite a man and woman together.

"No one wins all the time," she warned him.

"I've never lost yet," he said.

It was hard to rush through Lisieux again without pausing. It was raining, one of those summer storms that drench the streets and send everyone flying for cover. It was obviously not the moment to suggest that Jean-Louis accompany her to the small museum that faithfully recorded the steps to sanctity taken by the little Thérèse, so-called to distinguish her from the other great saint of her order, Teresa of Avilá.

There were signposts pointing this way and that, one to the overfurnished Victorian bourgeois home where Thérèse Martin was brought up, another to the convent where she ended her short life in her early twenties.

Jean-Louis surprised her then. "Do you want to stop?"

"May we?"

"I shouldn't have thought it was your kind of thing, but if you want to I don't mind taking a rest from driving in this rain."

She laughed out loud. "And who was always complaining about our weather in England?" she teased him.

"One day I'll take you to the department where I was born," he answered soberly. "The sun's always shining there. So far north, one might just as well be in England."

"Especially in Normandy," she agreed. "There are a lot of similarities, aren't there?"

"Are you trying to tell me you feel at home here?"

"Something like that," she admitted, surprising herself as much as him. How had it happened? She had only been here a matter of days! It took longer than that to put down roots in any place. Was it her father's influence? More likely Pierre's, she answered herself honestly. The truth was that she didn't want to go back to England, she wanted to stay in Normandy for the rest of her life.

"There's no such place as Normandy nowadays," Jean-Louis told her. "There are only the departments of Seine-Maritime, Eure, Orne, Calvados and Manche." He said it with a quiet satisfaction as if he were glad that some upstart had dismantled the old dukedom and tried to deprive it of its history.

So Normandy was a mirage, she thought as she got out of the car, huddling her raincoat about her; like her love for Pierre. With any luck when she took a good look at both, neither of them would be real, and she'd go back to her old life untouched and unscathed, as English as she'd always thought herself to be.

The small museum in the Carmel was both poignant and restrained. Stephanie looked long and hard at the tresses of toffee-coloured hair that had been shorn from St. Thérèse's head when she had been clothed and, better still, the school exercise books in which she had written the best-seller *L'Histoire d'une Âme*, the story of her spiritual pilgrimage to the heights of sanctity.

"I wouldn't have thought you'd be interested in all this," Jean-Louis murmured, longing to be gone.

"I like saints," Stephanie told him.

"As long as you don't have to live with them?"

Stephanie bought some postcards made from early photographs of the serious-eyed French girl, accepting them first in French and then changing her mind and asking for the prayers on the back to be in English for her friends back home.

"Want one?" she asked Jean-Louis, throwing back her head and poking out her tongue at him.

"No, thank you." He stared back at her. "I'm beginning to wonder what else I don't know about you," he said. "You're full of surprises today."

"If you knew me, you wouldn't like me at all," she comforted him, and then wondered if she'd said the wrong thing. There was a queer look in his eyes, as if he wasn't really listening to her at all, but to his own thoughts, and they weren't very pleasant thoughts to judge by the scowl on his face. "Hey, Jean-Louis! Your charm is slipping! I don't mind you liking me a little bit."

He turned on his heel and walked out into the street. "You can't have it both ways," he snapped. "If you don't want me, don't tease me."

She ran after him. "I'm sorry," she apologised.

He was his usual bland self by the time she caught up with him. "I'm sorry," she said again.

"It doesn't matter," he responded. "He who has the last laugh and all that. I've got it made, haven't I?"

Stephanie didn't answer him. If he hadn't known the real her, she reflected, perhaps she'd never known him either. Suddenly he seemed much more dangerous than she had ever thought him to be before. She wished the journey to Rouen over, but there was still more than half of it to come. She began to think she'd made a mistake asking Jean-Louis to drive her there. What would she do if he wouldn't leave her there when they arrived? She felt cold inside at the thought of quarreling with him in a strange town, with nobody around to help her.

It was a silent journey under grey, lowering skies. In the distance the thunder rumbled, sounding more menacing than usual. It was like an Alfred Hitchcock set, Stephanie thought, with herself cast as victim when one of those ordinary people turned out to be very extraordinary indeed!

She tried to relax and not to notice that, like so many Frenchmen, Jean-Louis drove faster than was wise on the busy road. She counted the yellow lozenges that told them they had priority over the usual rule of giving way to all traffic coming from the right, but she lost count almost as soon as she'd started. A little while later she realised she was shivering inside, that she was frightened of Jean-Louis and that she didn't know why. She checked the signposts to make sure they were still on the road for Rouen and chided herself for being a fool. Jean-Louis wouldn't hurt her. Why should he want to? But the feeling refused to go away. She kept remembering the look in his eyes she had witnessed at Lisieux. She made her mind a blank and a new thought came to her; Jean-Louis wouldn't be half as interested in her if he hadn't thought she wanted Pierre—and that Pierre wanted her! She chewed at her lower lip, wishing the thought away. Jean-Louis wouldn't do anything to upset his career. At least she could be sure of that!

Rouen came quickly in the end. One moment they seemed to have been on the road forever, and the next they were crossing the river and driving along the right bank of the Seine before they turned up for the cathedral.

"You can drop me anywhere here," Stephanie told him. "I'm hoping to book into the same hotel where I was before, and you can't take the car much nearer. I can carry my suitcase."

Jean-Louis didn't betray what he was thinking by moving so much as a muscle. He looked pleasant and clean, with his hair slicked back and as much under control as if he'd just put a comb through it. His hair was short and cut well away from his neck. Stephanie wondered why she had never noticed before that his homburg had put a kink in the ends. It was something, she supposed, that for once he wasn't wearing his bowler.

"I'll see you to your hotel," he said.

Stephanie was out of the car in a flash. "No, don't bother! I'll write and tell you my address." May she be forgiven, but that was the last thing she meant to do! She couldn't get rid of him fast enough.

"I wouldn't dream of leaving you here alone," he said. He put a coin in the parking meter, checked his watch and added another one. "We'll just have time before I have to leave for Paris."

"Time for what?" she demanded.

"To see you comfortably housed for the night, what else?"

Her imagination ran riot. She licked her lips to give herself time to think. "I don't want to delay you," she said at last.

He put his hand on her arm and picked up her suitcase, gesturing her to lead the way. "It won't hurt you to kiss me goodbye," he said in exactly the same tone as he had said everything else. "I'm entitled to a few kisses. I don't have to be in Paris until tomorrow. Why don't we have dinner together—"

"No!"

He smiled, a hateful smile that was wholly without amusement. "I thought you'd grown up—"

She seized her suitcase from his limp hand, her back rigid with shock. "Thank you for the lift, and no thank you for anything else!"

He laughed, enjoying himself. "You can carry the suitcase if you like, my dear. I'll follow."

Stephanie fumed with a rage that was partly directed towards herself. How had she managed to get into this? How was she going to get out of it? She tightened her grasp on the handle of her suitcase and quickened her steps until she was almost running.

"Are you planning to take refuge in the cathedral?" Jean-Louis' mocking voice came after her.

"What if I am?"

She sped towards the ornate entrance, swerved at the last moment and cut back through another building opposite and into the pedestrians only part of the city. There was an awkward moment when she had to wait at the lights to cross to the rue du Gros Horloge and she glanced back over her shoulder, more relieved than she could say when there was no visible sign of Jean-Louis following her.

The clock dominated the street, its one hand spelling out the time and reminding her it would soon be evening. She couldn't believe that Jean-Louis would do this to her. How dare he? He wouldn't have looked at her twice in England—even when they were engaged he'd done no more than kiss her as if she were a favourite child, except for once or twice, when it had always been she who had broken away, not really liking to be close to him.

Was she really so different now? When she thought about it the answer to that was obvious. She could sum it up in one word: Pierre. She groaned at the back of her throat, overcome with longing to see his tall, well-made figure as she had first seen him, coming towards her down the street.

Hardly aware that she had done so, she took a seat at the café where she'd been sitting then, and the same waitress came out to take her order. If she sat where she was for a while, she reasoned, Jean-Louis would have given up by the time she walked back past the cathedral and towards the hotel. She asked for a coffee, trying to ward off the miserable certainty that she was more lonely just then than she had ever been in her whole life. Why had she ever come away? At that moment her independence seemed a very poor thing. She would have given anything to have been back with her grandmother—and Pierre.

A man sitting in the shadows beyond her stood up, lifted the chair beside her into a more convenient place and sat down.

"What kept you?" Pierre asked.

Chapter Eleven

"Didn't you expect me?"

She shook her head wordlessly. A great wave of delight passed through her at the sight of him, leaving her weak and helpless and, for the moment, breathlessly happy.

Pierre grinned at her. "Pleased to see me?"

This time she nodded without any thought of dissembling. She had never been more glad to see anyone. She didn't know how it had come about but this man was as close to her as her own muscles and bones. Wasn't there something in the Bible about being one flesh? Now she knew what it meant.

"Still saying nothing?"

She allowed her eyes to rest on the opening in his scarlet shirt and made the most of the longing she had to touch him.

"What's there to say?" she said.

He glanced at his watch. "You, my darling, have a great deal of talking to do," he said firmly. "You have five minutes to explain why I shouldn't take a stick to you." His glance lingered on her open mouth. "Or why I shouldn't find a room somewhere and make passionate love to you until you admit it's me you want and not *him!*"

"I never have wanted him."

His eyebrows shot up. "Never? You were engaged to marry the man!"

"Yes, I was. It seemed like a good idea at the time."

"You were *dazzled* by him?"

"I might just as easily have been dazzled by some nice, safe film star," she murmured ruefully.

Pierre looked a little less like a lord of vengeance. He relaxed back into his chair and took a sip from her cup of coffee.

"And when did you make this earth-shattering discovery?" he enquired.

She was silent for a long time, wondering how to answer. Nothing had really changed by his being here—and yet why should she dissemble? She had nothing to hide. She had spent a perfectly hideous day trying to escape from Pierre and where had that got her? Precisely nowhere.

She smiled a slow, self-satisfied smile. "It was coming slowly to me anyway, but the moment when I knew was on the ferry coming over."

He looked as pleased as if she had given him an unexpected present. "I thought you were feeling too ill to be making any great discoveries?"

"I felt better after a while."

He relaxed still further. "A new interest perhaps?"

"Perhaps."

"This sounds interesting. Tell me more!"

She could feel the hot colour climbing up into her face and took a hasty sip of coffee to disguise the blush from him. If she told him any more it could only be at the sacrifice of her pride. Was she ready to do that? The cup clattered against its saucer as she put it down, betraying her nervousness.

"I'm not kidnapped every day of my life," she said, trying to put him off.

"You came willingly enough."

"Mmm." She had, she supposed. "I was curious—"

"About me?"

The heat in her cheeks grew hotter still. "About my brand-new grandmother!"

"Indeed?"

"She didn't speak very highly of you, if I remember rightly!" Stephanie told him with renewed spirit. "She said if you'd decided on a romantic interlude with someone, nobody, not even she, would be able to stop you! She spoke from experience no doubt?"

"She knew I had my eye on you?"

Stephanie bit her lip. "Did you?"

He leaned forward suddenly and she retreated backwards. "Didn't you notice?" he demanded.

"Y—yes, I noticed!"

"You knew you were mine yet you still ran away?"

Stephanie would have moved her hands onto the arms of her chair, but he was there before her, imprisoning her where she sat. She avoided meeting the fiery challenge in his dark eyes, demurely lowering her own to her lap.

"Yours?" she jerked out. "What makes you think that?"

He came nearer still. "If I told you that, *ma minette en sucre,* you'd do more than blush and, much as I like to see the effect I have on you, this is a public place—" He shrugged his shoulders in a Gallic gesture that clarified his meaning as no mere words could have done.

"I don't belong to anyone!" The words didn't come out in the shout of indignation she had planned, but in a whisper.

"I hope you told Jean-Louis that!"

She went on looking at her lap, pleating the material of her skirt with nervous fingers. "We stopped off at Lisieux." She shivered as she remembered the look on Jean-Louis' face when they had come out of the museum.

"Did he hurt you?"

"No." She took a rasping breath. "We went to the museum of St. Thérèse in the Carmel—"

"Yes, I remember. You wanted to go there before. Did it live up to your expectations?"

"I like saints," she said, just as she had said to Jean-Louis.

Pierre's lips hovered over hers, brushing them in a kiss so gentle that the tears started into her eyes.

"Did you put yourself under her protection, *ma vie?*"

"I've known Jean-Louis simply ages—"

"What did you do with him?"

"I lost him in front of the cathedral." She experienced again the relief she'd felt when she'd realised he was no longer following her. "He never really wanted me before, not that way. He wanted to go to the hotel with me. I can't understand it!"

Pierre's second kiss was as possessive as his first had been gentle. "I don't like your Jean-Louis," he said. "I don't like the look in his eyes."

She didn't either, but then she'd never noticed it before. "He's good at disguising his feelings. I suppose his job's taught him that. I could kick myself for being such a simpleton. I thought he was a gentleman—"

"So you said. Whereas I was merely a man!"

She sniffed, feeling better. "It was you who said I'd prefer the man in the end," she baited him.

His eyes lit. "That wasn't exactly what I said, but no matter. As long as you've woken up to Jean-Louis' methods, I'll forgive you the rest."

"Oh, will you? What is there to forgive?"

He ran his forefinger down the straight line of her nose. "A great deal. I told you not to go with him."

Her green eyes flashed. "You made a great many unnecessary, chauvinistic threats! What did you expect?"

"I expected you to listen to me. It was obvious what Jean-Louis was after. Tante Janine's manor house is a heritage to be proud of."

Stephanie shook her head with vigour. "My stepfather wasn't a poor man either."

"He'd no reason to leave his fortune to you, however. He didn't, did he?"

Stephanie put her head on one side. "I wish you'd known him," she said. "He told me long ago he was leaving everything to my mother, the love of his life, except a small competence which he wanted me to have, he said, because he'd figured it out and come to the conclusion that most of the big mistakes women make in their lives are because they have no financial independence, even now. He wanted me to be able to choose, no matter what happened to me. It isn't luxury, but it's enough to allow me to walk out on an unbearable situation."

"Your stepfather was a big man," Pierre commented.

Stephanie nodded. "He knew why Mother married him. I think she'd have married him anyway because she hates being on her own. I expect she'll marry again as soon as she can."

Pierre gave Stephanie a thoughtful look. "Are you trying to tell me Jean-Louis was meant to be more of a companion than a lover?"

"I'm telling you about my mother!" If she'd been telling him about herself she would have had to tell him about the other discovery she'd made, that in that respect she wasn't like her mother at all. If she couldn't have Pierre, then she wouldn't have anyone!

"Was he ever your lover?" Pierre shot through her thoughts.

She couldn't believe her ears. "Jealous?" she fired back at him.

He smiled wryly at her lifted chin. "What do you think?" he countered.

Was it possible? A new excitement uncurled itself in her abdomen. "I think," she said slowly, "I think you love your Tante Janine better than any other woman you know."

"Is that so?"

She nodded. "My attraction is my green eyes. Even I can see they're just like hers."

Pierre's smile grew broader. "You have other attractions," he said, adding, "And you flirt very nicely."

To the best of her knowledge she'd never flirted with anyone before. It gave her a sense of power that she was enjoying very much.

"Is that all you want from me? A flirtation?" she mocked him. "Or would you prefer an affair?"

"I'm in your hands," he said.

She took a deep breath. "I think I'd better book myself a room for the night—a *single* room—" He shook his head at her. "No?"

"No, my love, you're coming home with me. Didn't I tell you I'd drag you back by your hair if I had to?"

She sighed. "I couldn't have anything to do with someone who didn't take my career as seriously as his own."

"You can paint all you want once we've got this other out of the way!" he exclaimed.

"I'm due at the Art School tomorrow morning."

"I've cancelled your appointment."

The excitement died, to be replaced by a very real anger. "You did what?"

"I postponed your start at the school until after we'd got things straight between us. You've no reason to object to that. You knew I wasn't going to let you go—"

She ground her teeth. "Because of Grandmère?

She understood why I was going. She knew I'd visit all I could. If she's your excuse, think again, Pierre!"

"This has nothing to do with Tante Janine. This is between us. You knew that, *ma chère* Stephanie. You've known it all along. You threw down a challenge and I picked it up. Now you'll have to take the consequences, and the first one is that you'll be a term late joining your art classes."

"The first?"

"I'll tell you about the others on the way home."

Her eyes grew very large and round. "We're going to England?"

His fingers bit into her upper arms. "Is that meant to be another challenge?" he demanded.

She took fright. "I take it back!" she surrendered.

"You're coming home with me?"

She was not a gambler by nature, and it cost her a lot to take such a big risk now. Not that she had any choice. The stake had been her whole future for a long time now. She hadn't called it and, in fairness, she had to admit that he hadn't either. He didn't know even now that he held the essence of her being in the palm of his hand.

She inclined her head very slowly. "Yes, I'm coming home with you," she agreed.

He relaxed his hold on her, the light in his eyes softening into a warmth that drowned the last of her doubts.

"Was that so hard to say? It's saved us both a great deal of trouble." He put a hand on her hair and gave it a gentle tug.

She looked an enquiry. "Trouble?"

"I meant what I said. No way was Jean-Louis going to have you."

She felt obliged to make some kind of protest. "What about my freedom of choice?"

"You made your choice when you got in my car and came with me to meet your French grandmother."

"Ah," she said, "so that's when I made my mistake. I thought you kidnapped me to please your Tante Janine."

Despite her best efforts to sound cool and amused, she was afraid that the niggling worry at the back of her mind came through, and she knew he was discerning enough where she, was concerned to pick it up.

He did. "Tante Janine was the only one of my relatives ever to do anything for me. I owe her an awful lot. But I'm my own man, *chérie*. I was when she took me in, and I am now. *Mon oncle* insisted I take his surname—it was a matter of pride, I think— but I've never been an Anders. Tante Janine and I met as friends and she's never wanted it any other way, not even when I was twelve years old and facing up to the loss of both parents and the life I'd known up to then. I sought you out for her sake, to encourage you to visit her—I kidnapped you for my own."

The happiness within her bubbled up into a laugh. "You must have peculiar tastes to settle for a seasick, jilted—"

"Just as well," Pierre said. "If you'd been engaged to him it wouldn't have made any difference."

Her laughter died and she looked at him in awe. "Do you want me as much as that?"

He gave her back look for look. "Didn't you know?" He stood up, easing her to her feet, and picked up her suitcase. "The sooner we get home the better," he said. "We've wasted enough time."

Genuine Silhouette sterling silver bookmark for only $15.95!

What a beautiful way to hold your place in your current romance! This genuine sterling silver bookmark, with the distinctive Silhouette symbol in elegant black, measures 1½" long and 1" wide. It makes a beautiful gift for yourself, and for every romantic you know! And, at only $15.95 each, including all postage and handling charges, you'll want to order several now, while supplies last.

Send your name and address with check or money order for $15.95 per bookmark ordered to
Simon & Schuster Enterprises
120 Brighton Rd., P.O. Box 5020
Clifton, N.J. 07012
Attn: Bookmark

Bookmarks can be ordered pre-paid only. No charges will be accepted. Please allow 4-6 weeks for delivery.

N.Y. State Residents
Please Add Sales Tax

Silhouette Romance

IT'S YOUR OWN SPECIAL TIME
Contemporary romances for today's women.
Each month, six very special love stories will be yours
from SILHOUETTE.

$1.75 each

☐ 100 Stanford	☐ 128 Hampson	☐ 157 Vitek	☐ 185 Hampson
☐ 101 Hardy	☐ 129 Converse	☐ 158 Reynolds	☐ 186 Howard
☐ 102 Hastings	☐ 130 Hardy	☐ 159 Tracy	☐ 187 Scott
☐ 103 Cork	☐ 131 Stanford	☐ 160 Hampson	☐ 188 Cork
☐ 104 Vitek	☐ 132 Wisdom	☐ 161 Trent	☐ 189 Stephens
☐ 105 Eden	☐ 133 Rowe	☐ 162 Ashby	☐ 190 Hampson
☐ 106 Dailey	☐ 134 Charles	☐ 163 Roberts	☐ 191 Browning
☐ 107 Bright	☐ 135 Logan	☐ 164 Browning	☐ 192 John
☐ 108 Hampson	☐ 136 Hampson	☐ 165 Young	☐ 193 Trent
☐ 109 Vernon	☐ 137 Hunter	☐ 166 Wisdom	☐ 194 Barry
☐ 110 Trent	☐ 138 Wilson	☐ 167 Hunter	☐ 195 Dailey
☐ 111 South	☐ 139 Vitek	☐ 168 Carr	☐ 196 Hampson
☐ 112 Stanford	☐ 140 Erskine	☐ 169 Scott	☐ 197 Summers
☐ 113 Browning	☐ 142 Browning	☐ 170 Ripy	☐ 198 Hunter
☐ 114 Michaels	☐ 143 Roberts	☐ 171 Hill	☐ 199 Roberts
☐ 115 John	☐ 144 Goforth	☐ 172 Browning	☐ 200 Lloyd
☐ 116 Lindley	☐ 145 Hope	☐ 173 Camp	☐ 201 Starr
☐ 117 Scott	☐ 146 Michaels	☐ 174 Sinclair	☐ 202 Hampson
☐ 118 Dailey	☐ 147 Hampson	☐ 175 Jarrett	☐ 203 Browning
☐ 119 Hampson	☐ 148 Cork	☐ 176 Vitek	☐ 204 Carroll
☐ 120 Carroll	☐ 149 Saunders	☐ 177 Dailey	☐ 205 Maxam
☐ 121 Langan	☐ 150 Major	☐ 178 Hampson	☐ 206 Manning
☐ 122 Scofield	☐ 151 Hampson	☐ 179 Beckman	☐ 207 Windham
☐ 123 Sinclair	☐ 152 Halston	☐ 180 Roberts	☐ 208 Halston
☐ 124 Beckman	☐ 153 Dailey	☐ 181 Terrill	☐ 209 LaDame
☐ 125 Bright	☐ 154 Beckman	☐ 182 Clay	☐ 210 Eden
☐ 126 St. George	☐ 155 Hampson	☐ 183 Stanley	☐ 211 Walters
☐ 127 Roberts	☐ 156 Sawyer	☐ 184 Hardy	☐ 212 Young

$1.95 each

☐ 213 Dailey	☐ 217 Vitek	☐ 221 Browning	☐ 225 St. George
☐ 214 Hampson	☐ 218 Hunter	☐ 222 Carroll	☐ 226 Hampson
☐ 215 Roberts	☐ 219 Cork	☐ 223 Summers	☐ 227 Beckman
☐ 216 Saunders	☐ 220 Hampson	☐ 224 Langan	☐ 228 King

READERS' COMMENTS ON SILHOUETTE ROMANCES:

"The best time of my day is when I put my children to bed at naptime and sit down to read a Silhouette Romance. Keep up the good work."

P.M.*, Allegan, MI

"I am very fond of the quality of your Silhouette Romances. They are so real. I have tried to read some of the other romances, but I always come back to Silhouette."

C.S., Mechanicsburg, PA

"I feel that Silhouette Books offer a wider choice and/or variety than any of the other romance books available."

R.R., Aberdeen, WA

"I have enjoyed reading Silhouette Romances for many years now. They are light and refreshing. You can always put yourself in the main characters' place, feeling alive and beautiful."

J.M.K., San Antonio, TX

"My boyfriend always teases me about Silhouette Books. He asks me, how's my love life and naturally I say terrific, but I tell him that there is always room for a little more romance from Silhouette."

F.N., Ontario, Canada

*names available on request